Cops before breakfast. Before coffee even...

Los Angeles bookseller and aspiring mystery author Adrien English's high school buddy (and employee) is stabbed to death in a back alley following a loud and very public argument with Adrien the previous evening.

Naturally the cops want to ask Adrien a few questions; they are none too impressed with his answers, and when a few hours later someone breaks into Adrien's shop and ransacks it, the law is inclined to think Adrien is trying to divert suspicion from himself.

Adrien knows better. Adrien knows he is next on the killer's list.

FATAL SHADOWS

THE ADRIEN ENGLISH MYSTERIES
BOOK ONE

JOSH LANYON

Fatal Shadows

The Adrien English Mysteries, Book 1

Revised edition, October 2014

ISBN: 978-1-937909-15-4

Printed in the United States of America

JustJoshin Publishing, Inc.

3053 Rancho Vista Blvd.

Suite 116

Palmdale, CA 93551

www.joshlanyon.com

This is a work of fiction. Any resemblance to persons living or dead is entirely coincidental.

TABLE OF CONTENTS

Life will show you masks that are worth all your carnivals.

Ralph Waldo Emerson, *Illusions*

CHAPTER ONE

Cops before breakfast. Before coffee even. As if Mondays weren't bad enough. I stumbled downstairs, unlocked the glass front doors, shoved back the ornate security gate and let them in: two plainclothes detectives.

They identified themselves with a show of badges. Detective Chan was older, paunchy, a little rumpled, smelling of Old Spice and cigarettes as he brushed by me. The other one, Detective Riordan, was big and blond, with a neo-Nazi haircut and tawny eyes. Actually I had no idea what color his eyes were, but they were intent and unblinking, as though waiting for a sign of activity from the mouse hole.

"I'm afraid we have some bad news for you, Mr. English," Detective Chan said as I started down the aisle of books toward my office.

I kept walking, as though I could walk away from whatever they were about to tell me.

"...concerning an employee of yours. A Mr. Robert Hersey."

I slowed, stopped there in front of the Gothic section. A dozen damsels in distress (and flimsy negligees) caught my eyes. I turned to face the cops. They wore what I would describe as "official" expressions.

"What about Robert?" There was a cold sinking in my gut. I wished I'd stopped for shoes. Barefoot and unshaven, I felt unbraced for bad news. Of course it was bad news. Anything to do with Robert was bound to be bad news.

"He's dead." That was the tall one, Riordan. He-Man.

"Dead," I repeated.

Silence.

"You don't seem surprised."

"Of course I'm surprised." I was, wasn't I? I felt kind of numb. "What happened? How did he die?"

They continued to eye me in that assessing way.

"He was murdered," Detective Chan said.

My heart accelerated, then began to slug against my ribs. I felt the familiar weakness wash through me. My hands felt too heavy for my arms.

"I need to sit down," I said.

I turned and headed back toward my office, reaching out to keep myself from careening into the crowded shelves. Behind me came the measured tread of their feet, just audible over the singing in my ears.

I pushed open my office door, sat heavily at the desk and opened a drawer, groping inside. The phone on my desk began to ring, jangling loudly in the paperback silence. I ignored it, found my pills, managed to get the top off, and palmed two. Washed them down with a swallow of whatever was in the can sitting there from yesterday. Tab. Warm Tab. It had a bracing effect.

"Sorry," I told L.A.'s Finest. "Go ahead."

The phone, which had stopped ringing, started up again. "Aren't you going to answer that?" Riordan inquired after the fourth ring.

I shook my head. "How did —? Do you know who —?"

The phone stopped ringing. The silence was even more jarring.

"Hersey was found stabbed to death last night in the alley behind his apartment," Chan answered.

Riordan said, without missing a beat, "What can you tell us about Hersey? How well did you know him? How long had he worked for you?"

"I've known Robert since high school. He's worked for me for about a year."

"Any problems there? What kind of an employee was he?"

I blinked up at Chan. "He was okay," I said, at last focusing on their questions.

"What kind of friend was he?" Riordan asked.

"Sorry?"

"Were you sleeping with him?"

I opened my mouth but nothing came out.

"Were you lovers?" Chan asked, glancing at Riordan.

"No."

"But you are homosexual?" That was Riordan, straight as a stick figure, summing me up with those cool eyes, and finding me lacking in all the right stuff.

"I'm gay. What of it?"

"And Hersey was homosexual?"

"And two plus two equals a murder charge?" The pills kicking in, I felt stronger. Strong enough to get angry. "We were friends, that's all. I don't know who Robert was sleeping with. He slept with a lot of people."

I didn't quite mean it that way, I thought as Chan made a note. Or did I? I still couldn't take it in. Robert murdered? Beaten up, yes. Arrested, sure. Maybe even dead in a car crash — or by autoerotic misadventure. But *murdered?* It seemed so unreal. So...Film At Eleven.

I kept wanting to ask if they were *sure*. Probably everyone they interviewed asked the same question.

I must have been staring fixedly into space because Riordan asked abruptly, "Are you all right, Mr. English? Are you ill?"

"I'm all right."

"Could you give us the names of Hersey's — uh — men friends?" Chan asked. The too-polite "men friends" put my teeth on edge.

"No. Robert and I didn't socialize much."

Riordan's ears pricked up. "I thought you were friends?"

"We were. But —"

They waited. Chan glanced at Riordan. Though Chan was older I had the impression that Riordan was the main man. The one to watch out for.

I said cautiously, "We were friends, but Robert worked for me. Sometimes that put a strain on our relationship."

"Meaning?"

"Just that we worked together all day; we wanted to see different people at night."

"Uh huh. When was the last time you saw Mr. Hersey?"

"We had dinner —" I paused as Chan seemed about to point out that I had just said Robert and I didn't socialize. I finished lamely, "And then Robert left to meet a friend."

"What friend?"

"He didn't say."

Riordan looked skeptical. "When was this?"

"When was what?"

Patiently, long-suffering professional to civilian, he re-phrased, "When and where did you have dinner?"

"The Blue Parrot on Santa Monica Blvd. It was about six."

"And when did you leave?"

"Robert left about seven. I stayed and had a drink at the bar."

"You have no idea who he left to meet? A first name? A nickname?"

"No."

"Do you know if he was going home first or if they were meeting somewhere?"

"I don't know." I frowned. "They were meeting somewhere, I think. Robert looked at his watch and said he was late; it would take him ten minutes. If he had been heading back home it would have taken him half an hour."

Chan jotted all this in the small notebook.

"Anything else you can tell us, Mr. English? Did Mr. Hersey ever indicate he was afraid of anyone?"

"No. Of course not." I thought this over. "What makes you think he wasn't mugged?"

"Fourteen stab wounds to his upper body and face."

I felt the blood drain out of my brain again.

"Those kinds of wounds generally indicate prior acquaintance," Riordan drawled.

I don't remember exactly all they asked, after that. Irrelevant details, I felt at the time: Did I live alone? Where had I gone to school? How long had I owned the shop? What did I do with my spare time?

They verified the spelling of my name. "Adrien, with an 'e'," I told Chan. He almost, but not quite, smirked.

They thanked me for my cooperation, told me they would be in touch.

Before he left my office, Riordan picked up the empty can on my desk. "Tab. I didn't know they still made that."

He crushed it in one powerful fist and tossed it in the trash basket.

* * * * *

The phone started ringing before I could relock the front door. For a moment I thought it was Robert calling in sick again.

"Adrien, *mon chou,*" fluted the high, clear voice of Claude La Pierra. Claude owns Café Noir on Hillhurst Ave. He's big and black and beautiful. I've known him about three years. I'm convinced he's a Southland native, but he affects a kind of gender-confused French like a Left Bank expatriate with severe memory loss. "I just heard. It's too ghastly. I still can't believe it. Tell me I'm dreaming."

"The police just left."

"The *police? Mon Dieu!* What did they say? Do they know who did it?"

"I don't think so."

"What did they tell you? What did you tell them? Did you tell them about me?"

"No, of course not."

A noisy sigh of relief quivered along the phone line. "*Certainement pas!* What is there to tell? But what about *you?* Are you all right?"

"I don't know. I haven't had time to think."

"You must be in shock. Come by for lunch."

"I can't, Claude." The thought of food made me want to vomit. "I — there's no one to cover."

"Don't be so *bourgeois.* You have to eat, Adrien. Close the shop for an hour. *Non!* Close it for the day!"

"I'll think about it," I promised vaguely.

No sooner had I hung up on Claude than the phone rang again. I ignored it, padding upstairs to shower.

But once upstairs I sank on the couch, head in my hands. Outside the kitchen window I could hear a dove cooing, the soft sound distinct over the mid-morning rush of traffic.

Rob was dead. It seemed both unbelievable and inevitable. A dozen images flashed through my brain in a macabre mental slide show: Robert at sixteen, in his West Valley Academy tennis whites. Robert and me, drunk and fumbling, in the Ambassador Hotel the night of the senior prom. Robert on his wedding day. Robert last night, his face unfamiliar and distorted by anger.

No chance now to ever make it up. No chance to say goodbye. I wiped my eyes on my shirt sleeve, listened to the muffled ring of the phone downstairs. I told myself to get up and get dressed. Told myself I had a business to run. I continued to sit there, my mind racing ahead, looking for trouble. I could see it everywhere, looming up, pointing me out of the lineup. Maybe that sounds selfish, but half a lifetime of getting myself out of shit Robert landed me in had made me wary.

For seven years I had lived above the shop in Old Pasadena. Cloak and Dagger Books. New, used and vintage mysteries, with the largest selection of gay and gothic whodunits in Los Angeles. We held a workshop for mystery writers on Tuesday nights. My partners in crime had finally convinced me to put out a monthly newsletter. And I had just sold my own first novel, *Murder Will Out*, about a gay Shakespearean actor who tries to solve a murder during a production of *Macbeth*.

Business was good. Life was good. But especially business was good. So good that I could barely keep up with it, let alone work on my next book. That's when Robert had turned up in my life again.

His marriage to Tara, his (official) high school sweetheart, was over. Getting out of the marriage had cost what Rob laughingly called a "queen's ransom." After nine years and two-point-five children he was back from the Heartland of America, hard up and hard on. At the time it seemed like serendipity.

On automatic pilot, I rose from the sofa, went into the bathroom to finish my shower and shave, which had been interrupted by the heavy hand of the law on my door buzzer at 8:05 a.m.

I turned on the hot water. In the steamy surface of the mirror I grimaced at my reflection, hearing again that condescending, "But you *are* a homosexual?" As in, "But you *are* a lower life form?" So what had Detective Riordan seen? What was the first clue? Blue eyes, longish dark hair, a pale bony face. What was it in my Anglo-Norman ancestry that shrieked "faggot"?

Maybe he had a gaydar anti-cloaking device. Maybe there really was a straight guy checklist. Like those "How to Recognize a Homosexual" articles circa the Swinging '60s. Way back when I'd one stuck to the fridge door with my favorite give-aways highlighted:

Delicate physique (or overly muscular)

Striking unusual poses

Gushy, flowery conversation, i.e., "wild," "mad," etc.

Insane jealousy

What's funny about that? Mel, my former partner, had asked irritably, ripping the list down one day.

Hey, isn't that on the list? "Queer sense of humor?" Mel, *do you think I'm homosexual?*

So what led Detective Riordan to (in a manner of speaking) finger me? Still on automatic pilot, I got in the shower, soaped up, rinsed off, toweled down. It took me another fifteen numb minutes to find something to wear. Finally I gave up, and I dressed in jeans and a white shirt. One thing that will never give me away is any sign of above-average fashion sense.

I went back downstairs. Reluctantly.

The phone had apparently never stopped ringing. I answered it. It was a reporter: Bruce Green from *Boytimes*. I declined an interview and hung up. I plugged in the coffee machine, unlocked the front doors again, and phoned a temp agency.

CHAPTER TWO

"Silence equals death." This was Rob's favorite quote when I'd ask him not to come out (or on) to customers.

I'm running a business, not a political forum here, Rob.

You can't separate being gay from the rest of your life, Adrien. Everything a gay man does makes a political statement. Everything matters: where you bank, where you shop, where you eat. When you hold your lover's hand in public — oh, that's right...

Go to hell, Rob.

And his smile. That wicked grin so at odds with his golden boy good looks.

Reminders of his presence were everywhere. A rude sketch on a note I'd left him. Sunday's *Times* folded open to the half-finished crossword puzzle. A bag of pistachio nuts spilled on the counter.

I turned on the stereo in the stockroom, and music flooded the store aisles. Brahms's *Violin Concerto*: sweet and melancholy and incongruous with the idea of Robert hacked to death in an alley.

Despite the music it was too quiet. And cold. I shivered. It was an old building, originally a tiny hotel called The Huntsman's Lodge, built back in the '30s. I'd first stepped through its doors on a foggy spring day not long after I'd inherited what my mother refers to as "my money."

I remembered the echo of our footsteps as Mel and I wandered through the empty rooms with the real estate agent. We could have been in two different buildings.

Mel had seen the holes in the walls, the scarred wooden floors, the money pit. I'd looked past the peeling wallpaper, and the bare and flickering light bulbs in the watermarked ceiling to see the sagging staircase peopled by ghosts from the black and white movies of my childhood. Women in hats and gloves, men with cigarette holders clamped between jaunty smiles. I'd imagined them checking their valises and Gladstones at the mahogany lobby desk that now served as my sales counter. When the real estate agent casually mentioned there had been a murder here fifty years before, I was sold. Mel was resigned.

He must have seen the "S" for sucker stamped on your forehead.

Is that what that stands for? I thought it stood for something a bit more entertaining...

Followed by one of our brief wrestling matches, which ended unsurprisingly in Mel losing his temper.

Adrien, are you nuts? There's mouse crap everywhere.

Those were the good old days before I knew how much it cost to rewire a two-story building, or how the concept of modern plumbing has changed since the '30s. That was before I learned the hard way that you need more to compete with the low prices of Borders and Barnes and Noble let alone Amazon.com. Back before I learned there really is no such thing as Happily Ever After. But I did learn. I learned to stock backlist titles, to invest in variety and selection, to cater to the book groups, and reach out to the community. To put my heart and soul into my business. What I lacked in capital, I made up for in ambiance.

"Ambiance" meant placing comfortable old leather club chairs in strategic corners, "lighting" the fake fireplace on rainy days, and offering iced coffee during the summer. In our quest for ambiance, Mel and I raided local junk stores, lugging home an old gramophone, stacks of 78 records, kabuki theater masks, and a peacock fire screen. Ambiance earned us a write up in the *Times* Calendar Section, but it was hard work and long hours that kept me in business.

It was unusually quiet for a Monday morning. A couple of regulars browsed. A new face cleared the shop of all Joseph Hansen's Brandstetter series. Mrs. Lupinski brought in another sack of Harlequin Intrigues and tried to convince me they were real mysteries. I tackled the stuff Rob had left undone, feeling guilty for the lick of irritation over an unopened crate of hardbacks I'd purchased at an estate sale the previous weekend and the untouched stack of search lists he was supposed to check against the computer inventory.

I gathered up his scattered belongings. His coffee mug, which read, "Drink your coffee — people in Africa are sleeping." A couple of CDs. The razor and toothbrush he left in the washroom for those morning-afters. Most of it I packed in a box for his father, who lived now in a Huntington Beach nursing home.

I didn't want to keep playing it over in my mind, imagining what Rob's last moments must have been like. I bustled around facing books out, cutting strays out of the wrong shelves, pestering customers with offers of help and coffee. Over and over I asked myself the useless but inevitable *Why? Why Robert? Why kill him? Robbery? Maybe some coked up junkie?* The police said no. The police thought someone Robert knew had slain him. I heard again Detective Riordan's sardonic, "prior acquaintance." Did that mean Robert's killer was someone I also knew? I remembered Claude's anxious, "Did you tell them about me?" Was that the normal reaction of an innocent man?

It was hard to imagine stabbing a person fourteen times. I couldn't believe anyone I knew would be capable of that. Easier to believe it of a stranger, a hustler. Easier to believe Rob was the victim of a hate crime or random violence.

The day dragged. A few friends called asking about Rob, offering condolences, expressions of horror and sympathy, speculation.

About two o'clock, the silence got to me. I closed the shop and drove over to Claude's.

You can't miss Café Noir. Outside it's kitschy pink stucco, black grillwork and black shutters. Inside it's too dark to tell what the hell the decor might be. The floors are like black ice and just about as dangerous; the feathery outline of potted trees was barely discernable in the gloom.

Claude made clucking sounds when I walked in. He ushered me to one of the high back booths, promised to fix me something special and vanished. It was Monday and the café was officially closed, but Claude never seemed to leave the place.

I tried to relax. Tilted my head back and closed my eyes. Overhead Piaf trilled, *"Non, je ne regrette rien."* Easy for her to say.

After a time Claude reappeared and set a plate of linguine before me. The sharp-sweet scent of garlic and basil wafted from the tangle of pasta. He opened a bottle of wine, filled two glasses, and sat across from me.

"Have I ever told you, you look like Monty Clift?" he inquired in a deep, seductive voice.

"Before or after the accident?"

Claude tittered. Pushed my glass forward. "Red wine. Good for the heart."

"Thanks." I inhaled. "This smells heavenly."

"You need someone to look after you, *ma belle*." Claude wasn't smiling. With his sad, brown-velvet eyes he watched me spear a soft-shell crab bathed in tomato and herb sauce.

I took a bite. "I'm a born bachelor."

"Bah! You just need to meet Mr. Right."

This is one of Claude's favorite themes. In fact, it's a favorite theme with a lot of my friends. Gay and straight. Certain things are universal.

"Are you proposing?" I batted my eyelashes.

"Be serious," Claude insisted. "It's been how long since What's-His-Name walked? You've been alone so long you think it's normal. It's not normal. Everybody needs somebody —"

"Sometime?" I supplied helpfully. I twirled a forkful of linguine.

Claude sighed. Propped his chin on his gigantic paw. He watched me eat with an artist's satisfaction.

"So what really happened between you and Rob?" I asked.

"*Quelle est la question?* Fireworks then fizzle."

"So?" I took a sip of wine.

"So that was between me and Robert. Nobody else. I don't want cops fucking around in my life."

"That was — what? Six months ago? Why would the cops be more interested in you than anyone else?"

Claude's eyes slid away from mine. "I wrote him...letters, poems. Some of it was kind of...dark."

"No pun intended?"

Claude playfully slapped my hand. "I don't expect The Man to understand the creative mind."

"How dark *were* these poems and letters?"

"Pitch."

"Swell. You think Robert kept that stuff?"

Claude gnawed on his lower lip. "He could be sentimental. In the French sense."

What was the French sense? I rolled the wine over my tongue, savoring it, and considered Claude. "Who was Robert seeing after the two of you split up?"

"You should know."

I shot him a quick look. "Rob and I were never lovers."

Claude shrugged. One of those speaking Continental gestures. He didn't appear to be convinced. If Claude didn't believe me, did that mean other people suspected Rob and I were involved? And were they likely to share that suspicion with the cops? Watching me twist another forkful of pasta, he whispered hurriedly, "You could get those letters back, Adrien."

The fork froze a few centimeters from my lips. "Say again?"

"You've got a key to his place."

"Whoa, Nellie. Rob died in the alley behind that apartment building. It's a crime scene. Or as good as. The cops could be watching."

"Listen, *petit,* you're his best friend. Were. You're his boss. You could come up with a legitimate excuse for going over there."

"No. No. No."

"I wouldn't ask if it wasn't —"

"Read my lips. *Non.*"

Claude fell silent, gazing at me reproachfully.

I lowered my fork. "Is that why you asked me over here?"

"*Absolument pas!* The idea!"

"Yeah, right."

He bit his lip. I shook my head. His dimples showed.

* * * * *

I unlocked the side door to the shop. Pushed it open against an unexpected weight.

There were books everywhere: dumped in the aisles, scattered across the polished wood floor. A couple of shelves had been pulled over, the gramophone smashed to pieces beneath. The stack of Decca 78s had been sent flying like Frisbees. One had landed on top of a shelf. Another lay at my shoe tip like a black half-moon. I stooped to pick it up. Bing Crosby and The Andrews Sisters would never warble "Life Is So Peculiar" again.

My heart began to thud in a slow heavy pulse beneath my breastbone; the funny thing was that it was more in anger than fear. I took in the counter swept bare of everything except the computerized register, which was bolted into the mahogany. It was unplugged, its drawer open and empty. A coherent thought finally appeared. I went behind the counter, found the phone and dialed 911.

My call made, I put the phone back on the counter, took another look at the wreckage. I wanted to break something myself. That was when it occurred to me that whoever had broken in could still be hiding in the shop.

I grabbed the poker from the fireplace and headed for my office.

In the office the desk drawers had been pulled out and emptied, the file cabinet locks were broken, their contents dumped. My pills were crushed and sprinkled throughout the papers. Boxes of books, extra stock, now covered the wooden floor like crooked tiles of multicolored murder and mayhem. I slipped and slid my way across.

Poker raised, holding my breath, I stuck my head in the bathroom.

White tile, white porcelain, white paper towel dispenser — granted none of it as white as it could have been. The open window looked out on the alley behind the building.

I yanked the door forward.

No one lurked in the space between the door and the wall.

I backed out of the office and headed upstairs. The door to my flat was locked. Maybe there hadn't been time to pick the lock, but they had been up here. At the top of the stairs sat the grinning skull from the fireplace mantle below. Nice touch. A *memento mori*.

I made it halfway down the stairs before my legs gave out. I was still sitting there taking slow careful breaths when Detectives Chan and Riordan showed up.

Riordan stood surrounded by piles of books like Atlas or some bloke of equally mythic proportions: long legs encased in Levi's, powerful shoulders straining the seams of a surprisingly well-cut tweed jacket. He looked about himself dourly, all set to reject my application for the Good Housekeeping Seal of Approval.

Chan hiked up the stairs to me.

"Are you all right, Mr. English?"

"Fine."

"Coming back inside here was a bad idea, sir. You should have gone next door and called for help."

"Yeah, I realize that now."

"Can you tell us if anything appears to be missing?"

"Money from the register." I stared at the toppled shelves. Light flashed off the scattered pieces of glass from the broken mirror. Was that seven years of bad luck for my burglar or for me? I rubbed my forehead. "I don't know."

Chan observed me without speaking then turned away.

"They didn't break in." Riordan rejoined Chan at the foot of the stairs and they held a brief undervoiced conference.

"They must have used Robert's key," I said, digesting this. I thought of the bathroom window, but it was too small and too narrow, unless the burglar was a pygmy or a monkey.

Riordan glanced back. "Yeah, maybe."

"*Maybe?*"

Chan intervened, always urbane, easy. "Why don't you come downstairs where we can talk, Mr. English? Figure out if anything's missing. Figure out who might have done this."

Riordan said, "Give me your keys, Adrien. I'll check out upstairs. Make sure nobody's hiding under the bed."

"Rob didn't have a key to my apartment. And I'd have noticed if they'd kicked my door in."

"Let's just make sure, okay?"

I tossed my keys with more irritation than accuracy. Riordan caught them one-handed and stomped up the stairs past me. We heard him reach the landing. Heard the scrape of the key in the lock. Heard the creak of floorboards as he walked overhead.

Chan took out a stick of gum and folded it into his mouth.

In a few minutes Riordan was back with us. I saw him exchange one of those looks with Chan. He lifted a fake Chippendale chair to its feet, shoved it forward. I ignored the invitation.

"You don't look so hot, Adrien."

"Yeah, well I'm having a bad heart day."

His upper lip curled in a semblance of a smile. "Tell me about it."

I decided I would. "My best friend was murdered last night. My shop was burglarized today. This may be routine for you. It's not for me."

"Well," he drawled, "let's talk about that. About *Rob*. You didn't tell us everything this morning, did you?"

There was something different in their faces, in their voices, in the way Riordan was calling me "Adrien" instead of "Mr. English." It started the hairs on the back of my neck prickling.

"I'm not sure what you mean."

Riordan smiled. Lots of perfect white teeth, like a shark who saw his dentist regularly. Chan said, "We were just over at the Blue Parrot, interviewing the bartender when your call came over the radio. We thought we'd clear up a couple of points with you."

"Such as why you lied."

My head jerked puppet-like toward Riordan. "Lied?" I echoed.

"The bartender at The Blue Parrot said that you and the vic —" Chan corrected himself. "You and Mr. Hersey quarreled during your dinner, and that Mr. Hersey walked out and left you to pick up the check."

"I … invited Robert."

"I don't think that's the point, do you, Adrien?" Riordan inquired. He picked up a copy of *China House*, studied the two men embracing on the cover, snorted, and tossed it onto an empty shelf. "Why didn't you tell us you had a fight with Robert?"

"It wasn't a fight. It was a ... disagreement."

"And eight hours later the garbage men find what's left of the disagreeable Robert in a dumpster."

Distantly I wondered if I was going to pass out right there at their feet. Cold sweat was breaking out all over my body.

"You think *I* killed Rob?"

"There's a thought. Did you?"

"No."

"Sure?"

"Of course I'm sure!"

"Just relax, Mr. English," Detective Chan said. "These are routine questions, you know."

"What did you disagree about, you and *Rob*?"

I scrutinized Riordan. His eyes were hazel, I realized.

"About work," I said. "I felt like Rob didn't take it seriously. He was late, he left early. Sometimes he never showed at all. I'd give him stuff to do and he wouldn't do it. Petty stuff. I regret it now."

"Regret what?" Chan asked alertly.

"Regret arguing with him. Regret our last conversation being a fight over —" Tears itched down my cheeks. I wiped them away fast, knowing what these two would make of a grown man weeping.

"The bartender says before he walked out, Hersey yelled, "If I'm a thief, fire me." What did he mean by that?"

I viewed them. Chan was chewing gum tempestuously, studying his notepad. He looked tired, but his pudgy lined face was kindly. Riordan on the other hand.... How old was he? Thirty-five? Forty-five? He looked like a guy who expected the worst of people and was rarely disappointed.

"There was money missing from petty cash a couple of times."

"And you thought Hersey might have taken it?"

"I just wanted to hear his answer."

"Did you believe him?"

"Yes, of course."

Riordan laughed; a hard sound. "Why lie about that?" he asked. "If you lie about the little things, why should we believe you about the big things?"

"He was my *friend.*"

He lifted one shoulder. "People kill their friends. They kill their wives, their husbands, their mothers, fathers, sisters, brothers. They murder their own children. You have to do better than that."

"The most I would have done is fire him, and I wouldn't have fired him. Why the hell would I murder him? For pinching the petty cash? For being late? Jesus! And you're supposed to be detectives?"

Chan said soothingly, "Sure, you were friends a long time, you and Mr. Hersey. You were best man at his wedding, and when he came back to L.A. you gave him a job and helped him find a place to live. And became lovers. Again."

"We were never lovers."

"That's not the way we hear it," Riordan said. "We heard you and Rob were hump buddies from way back when Hersey used to cheat off your chemistry exams."

It occurred to me that I had it all wrong in my book. My cops were too abrasive. Riordan and Chan were courteous and careful. So when the contempt slipped out it was as shocking as a fist in the face.

I said as calmly and quietly as I could, "Robert left before I did last night. He left to meet someone. Didn't the bartender confirm that?"

Chan snapped his gum. "Sure did. Robert left at 6:45 and you stayed and had a second Midori margarita. You left about 7:30. Fifteen minutes later Robert showed up again looking for you."

CHAPTER THREE

Tara called that night.

"Tara," I floundered, when I recognized the tight voice on the other end of the line. "I was going to call you."

Two months after Rob split, Tara had miscarried their third child. It made a painful situation worse. It also made for stiff conversations the few times I had been unlucky enough to field her calls.

In my mind's eye I could see her as clearly as if I were studying a page in my high school yearbook: tall and slender, pale blue eyes, long blonde hair. The girl who is always picked to play the Virgin Mary in the Christmas pageant.

"You killed him." Her voice was so low I almost couldn't hear her. When I realized what she had said I felt my hair stand on end.

"What are you talking about?"

"You killed him just as surely as if you'd stuck the knife in his chest."

"Look, Tara, I know you're upset."

"You're the reason he came back here."

"He came back here because his family's here. Because he grew up here. Because his friends are here."

"Because *you're* here, Adrien, you faggot. You *pervert.* Do you think I don't *know?* Do you think Bob didn't tell me about you?"

The acid in her voice should have melted the phone line. I didn't know what to say. What the hell had Rob told her? "We were friends, that's all, Tara."

"Bullshit! *Bullshit.* We were happy, Adrien. Everything was going great for us. We had a great house. Great kids. A great life. Then you had to come along and screw it all up again." She sounded like she was crying. Hell.

"Tara, please believe me. Rob called *me.* I never — I sent a Christmas card every year. To both of you. That's it. That's the only contact I tried to make."

"LIAR!"

I held the phone away listening to her scream, "You are a goddamn liar, Adrien. You've ruined my life and you've killed Bob, so I hope you're happy. No, you know what I *really* hope, Adrien? I hope you die of AIDS. I hope you die with your body rotting and your brain eaten away...."

* * * * *

I shoved the sofa in front of the door, fixed a double brandy and fell asleep watching *The Crimson Pirate* with Burt Lancaster. But even the vision of Burt in his molded red and white striped breeches couldn't cheer me.

It's never fun knowing another human hates your guts, and I couldn't shake the feeling that I had wronged Tara. Not in the way she thought, but I felt guilty all the same.

About three o'clock in the morning I woke from chaotic dreams to find the lights on and the TV blasting infomercials. I turned off the television and lights, and dragged myself to bed. But once I'd lain down my brain kicked into high gear, and I kept reliving that final scene with Rob.

* * * * *

To say everything looked brighter in the morning would be an overstatement. For one thing it was pouring rain. Water rolled along the eaves like silver beads and poured off the striped awning. By mid-morning the streets were flooding. You feel rain in a used bookstore. The old pages pick up the damp and mustiness like old bones do rheumatism.

I dug out the powder blue cashmere cardigan my mother, Lisa, gave me the Christmas before last, pulled on my oldest, softest Levi's. Comfort clothes, the next best thing to a hug from a warm, living body. Lately there had been a shortage of hugs in my life. Lately there had been a shortage of warm, living bodies.

It was hard not to be depressed at the sight of yesterday's assault. Although I'd got the shelves back up with the help of the people who owned the Thai restaurant next door, the empty bookcases and bare walls were a chilling reminder. Suppose I'd walked in on the guy mid-rampage? There are things you can't insure against. Freaking lunatics are one of them.

The temp agency sent over Angus "Gus" Gordon. Angus was a pale, gangly twenty-something with John Lennon specs and a wispy goatee. Whether Angus had heard about Rob's murder and was unnerved by it, or whether he was just neurotically shy, he seemed unable to meet my eyes for longer than a second. His voice was so soft I had to ask him to repeat himself every time he spoke.

I put him to work stacking books back on the shelves. I didn't care if he couldn't alphabetize. Hell, I didn't care if he couldn't read. I just didn't want to be alone in the shop.

In the back office, I waded through the drifts of papers: catalogs, old receipts, invoices, shipping documents. Nothing seemed to be missing. There was nothing of value to anyone except possibly the IRS. It felt like the place had been trashed out of spite. I didn't see why this burglar should have such a grudge against me, but maybe it wasn't personal. Just an animal instinct for destruction.

The most unnerving thing was that I knew the police, as represented by Detectives Chan and Riordan, figured I'd faked a break-in to divert suspicion from myself. As Riordan put it, "This seems like a lot of trouble for sixty bucks in loose cash."

"You don't think this is connected with Robert's murder?" I'd demanded.

"Oh, I'm sure it's connected." he said obliquely.

"Were Rob's keys found?"

Riordan said reluctantly, as though it caused him physical pain to part with information, "No. There were no keys on the body or on the premises."

Which to his little gray cells could mean that I'd taken them away with me after I'd finished carving up my old "hump buddy."

The only reason I wasn't already sitting in jail watching Oprah was the cops hadn't finished building a slam dunk case against me. Imminent arrest, like their stale aftershave, hung in the air following Chan and Riordan's reluctant departure. They'd cautioned me about remaining available for further questioning.

I had a locksmith in before lunch to change the locks. The paper came and I read the details of "West Hollywood Man Murdered," sitting on the floor amid my sorting. According to the *L.A. Times*, thirty-three-year-old Robert Hersey had been found in the early hours of Monday, February 22nd, by sanitation workers making their daily rounds. Hersey had been stabbed repeatedly in the face, throat, and torso by an unknown assailant. The murder weapon had not been recovered. Police had questioned an unidentified man observed arguing with Hersey hours before his murder, but had made no arrest. "We are still trying to determine the identity of a man Hersey allegedly met later that evening," stated LAPD Detective Paul Chan.

A hoarse whisper from behind had me starting up off the floor. Angus stood there, glasses glinting blindly.

"Jeez! Don't do that!"

He was silent for a moment and then croaked, "Can I go to lunch now?"

"Yeah, of course. What time is it?"

"Noon."

"Okay."

Angus didn't budge. I felt a tickle between my shoulder blades — as though a knife were aimed at my back.

"How long do I get?"

"What?"

"How long can I take for lunch?" he whispered patiently.

"Oh. An hour, I guess."

I leaned back, watching him walk through the aisles of books, then I got up, stepped out of the office to see him go through the glass doors past the locksmith busily drilling away.

The phone rang and I picked it up. It was Bruce Green, the reporter from *Boytimes*.

"Don't hang up, Mr. English," he said right off the bat.

"Why not?"

"Because I'm trying to help you. My informant tells me LAPD plans to make you the scapegoat for Hersey's murder."

My finger hovered over the disconnect button, but I waited.

"You're gay and that's good enough for LAPD."

"I don't believe that," I said. I didn't know if I believed it or not. "Anyway, you're wasting your time. I don't know anything. I didn't kill Robert; that's the only thing I know."

"You'd better talk to somebody, Mr. English. Tell your story," advised Green. "Your next interview with Riordan and Chan will be downtown, take my word for it. They plan to have an arrest by the end of the week."

I tried to speak around the heart suddenly lodged in my throat. "What is it you think you can do for me?"

"I can get the support of the gay community behind you. We'll put your story on the front page: the story of how LAPD is trying to railroad an inno-cent gay man because they're too prejudiced and lazy to do their job."

I thought of "my story" on the front page, my photo in smudgy black and white, and I quailed.

"Mr. Green, I appreciate what you're trying to do, but I don't have any-thing to say."

"Just talk to me, Mr. English. Five minutes. That's all. Off the record."

"No. Really. Thank you, but no."

"You're making a mistake, Mr. English. Sooner or later —"

"Thank you, Mr. Green, but no thank you." I pressed disconnect.

I went behind the counter and started dialing customers whose search lists we'd matched. There was a 1972 first edition of Robert Bentley's *Here There Be Dragons* which had taken nine months to locate, and which I was tempted to keep for myself. A paperback copy of Ngaio Marsh's *When in Rome*, several Patricia Wentworth hardcovers: Ah, the thrill of the hunt!

The locksmith finished up and gave me the new keys. I paid him. A few customers wandered in and then straight out again, put off by our new and highly original floor display. I checked Angus's reshelving of the books and was relieved to see he could alphabetize.

After Angus returned from lunch I boiled water for Cup-a-Soup and returned to sorting through the piles and piles of paper littering the office. A forest's worth of bills, catalogs, bibliographies, press releases. It seemed as good a time as any to purge the files, do the spring cleaning I'd been putting off for the past couple of years.

It had been nearly twenty-four hours since I'd heard from Chan and Riordan. No news was good news, I told myself, and hoped it was true.

I was afraid the reporter from *Boytimes* was right, that with me as a convenient scapegoat, the police weren't interested in looking further. Motive and Opportunity. Those are the main two angles in any criminal homicide investigation. Since I had no alibi after leaving the Blue Parrot, the police would certainly conclude I had opportunity. Now they were hunting for motive. I was afraid that motive might be subjective.

I wondered if I needed to get hold of a lawyer? There was always the family firm. I tried to picture the ultra-conservative institution of Hitchcock & Gracen defending me in a homo *crime d'passionale* (as Claude would say), and wondered if it might not be easier to just shut up and go to prison. On the bright side, since Lisa only read the Society pages and the Calendar section, chances were she'd never hear anything about this, barring my arrest. For all I knew, I might be able to stall her through the first couple of years of my sentence with the skillful use of phone messages. *Do they let you keep your cell phone in prison?*

I sound more flippant than I felt. Each time I considered the real threat of arrest — *jail* — my brain seemed to flatline.

Angus turned out to be a hard worker. By late afternoon, he had half the books back on the shelves. Another day or two and we would be back in business for real.

Bundled in an army fatigue jacket, he appeared in the doorway of the office.

"Mr. English?" he mumbled, addressing the shelf above my head. "I'm going now."

I rose, dusting my knees off. "Sure." I looked at my watch. "Oh, sorry. You should have told me it was so late."

"Do you want me tomorrow?"

"Well, yeah. I mean, if you want to come back."

He gazed at me, owlish and unsmiling. "I like it here."

"Good. Then I'll see you tomorrow."

I walked him out, locked the door behind him. Maybe he was just socially backward. Maybe it was his first job.

Maybe I was imagining things.

*　*　*　*　*

On Tuesdays, the Partners in Crime mystery writers group usually met in the store after hours to critique each other's work in progress, tear published writers' books apart, and argue hot topics like who was bringing what refreshments next time.

That evening I half-expected, half-hoped everyone would cancel. It didn't happen. In fact all five members showed up early, with Claude arriving first. He wore a white raincoat, looking as suave as Shaft at a New Orleans funeral.

"*Mon chou,* have you reconsidered what we discussed yesterday?" He helped me set chairs in a semi-circle: a fake Chippendale, a fake Sheraton, and four genuine folding metal that pinched your butt if you didn't sit up straight. Cheap thrills.

We dragged the long library table to the center.

"If you're still talking career ops in B & E, no."

Claude made distressed noises.

"I can't believe you're serious about this," I said. "The police already suspect me."

"*You!*"

"*Moi.* Even if I —"

We were interrupted by the arrival of Jean and Ted Finch.

"Adrien, you poor baby!" exclaimed Jean, giving me a hug.

The Finches are writing partners, which seems like a surefire way to destroy a healthy marriage, but what do I know? My social life was pronounced DOA many moons ago. She's small and slim and dark, and so is he;

a matched pair, like bookends. They met at one of the Bouchercon mystery conferences. Love among the midlist.

"It's raining cats and dogs!" Ted announced, which gives you an idea of the sort of thing they write. He collapsed a rain-spotted red umbrella, adding, "We were sorry to hear about Rob, Adrien."

"Thanks." I felt awkward in my role as bereaved.

Jean, spotting Claude at the coffee maker, darted away to contest his decision to serve Godiva Cinnamon Hazelnut over Don Francisco's Moka Java.

Ted sidled over to me. "Do the police know who did it?"

"I don't think so. I'm not exactly in their confidence."

"Jean thinks it's a serial killer preying on the gay community."

"A serial killer with only one victim?"

"It has to start with someone."

I was still mulling over that happy thought when tall, well-built Max Siddons blew in. Max threw off his yellow poncho, shook himself like a dog, and made straight for the coffee and the chocolate pecan brownies provided by Jean. She giggled nervously as he flirted with her.

None of that awkward sentimental stuff for Max. I remembered that Robert had hit on Max once or twice when Rob first came back to L.A. That was before the thing with Claude. Rob had briefly joined our writing group but gave it up after we ran out of eligible men. Max was aggressively heterosexual which Robert had been convinced was just a facade. I never knew exactly what happened, but Max was coldly civil to Robert after the misunderstanding. Luckily duels were no longer acceptable social behavior.

Studying Max as he flattered Jean out of one side of his mouth and crammed brownies into the other, I wondered just how offended he had been.

Max finished grazing and sat down with Ted. They held a breezy postmortem over Rob. Ghoulish but probably inevitable with mystery writers. Wasn't I standing here considering whether muscular Max would be capable of tossing Robert's body into a trash dumpster? I shoved aside that mental picture, but as I went to get more pens I could still hear Max and Ted — now joined by Jean — comparing their theories against the newspapers' conjecture. As they knowledgeably debated the possibilities of disorganized lust murder over organized lust murder, and demonstrated their technical expertise by discussing types of blades, defense wounds, stab vs. slash injuries, I realized that Rob's death wasn't real for them. They could have been playing a grisly version of Clue.

"Are we going to get any work done tonight?" Grania Joyce demanded while I was in the storeroom.

"If Adrien ever stops futzing around," Max returned easily.

"I'm ready." I left the storeroom, pens in hand and joined them at the circle. Grania, head bent over her manuscript, reached for a pen without looking up. She's tall, red-haired, the Boadicea type. She turns out hard-boiled feminist stuff and informs me regularly that my writing is "anemic." Tonight she wore a T-shirt that proclaimed, *Listen to Girls*, which we did, settling down to the dissection of the first three chapters of Claude's *The Eiffel Tower Affaire* with huffy rustles of paper and under-breath comments from Max.

Robert's funeral was Friday.

It was one of those perfect days when the Santa Ana winds sweep the smog out over the ocean; the sky looked as uncannily blue as if it had been colorized by Ted Turner.

The mourners didn't outnumber the church officials by many. I recognized a few people but most were strangers. Strange to me anyway. Rob had always been popular. Where were the people we had gone to school with? The friends who, like me, stood by while he married Tara in a chapel very similar to this one? Where was all the extended family? The aunts, uncles, cousins? Where were the cronies of the last few liberated months? Claude did not show. Nor any of Robert's numerous lovers — at least none that I recognized.

The media were represented by a local news van parked by the cemetery gates. The murder of one gay man was hardly a Stop-the-Presses event. A bored reporter waited outside the vaulted-ceiling chapel kicking pebbles back and forth. There were a few sightseers. And, of course, the police. Detectives Chan and Riordan looked suitably grave in dark suits and sunglasses. I think I did a kind of guilty double take when I spotted them. Chan nodded affably.

I found a place behind Robert's father, shrunken in his wheelchair, and Robert's sisters. The younger one had had a crush on me in junior high. She could barely meet my eyes now.

Tara sat on the other side of the first row of pews, the kids with her, wide-eyed and scared. She looked like hell beneath her chic Princess Diana hat. Like she hadn't slept in days. That made two of us.

My mind kept wandering during the generic service. It was obvious the minister had never met Robert. Rob's sisters took turns getting up and speaking huskily about his qualities as a brother and husband and father and son. The church felt stuffy, airless. I viewed the rosewood casket. How quickly, how neatly the chaos of a living person could be reduced to an insignificant box.

When the service ended I hung back while everyone shuffled outside into the windy, sunlit afternoon. I wasn't sure how Tara would react to my presence. I didn't feel up to hysterics: hers or mine.

"Adrien? Mr. English?"

I turned around. Next to me stood a very tall man with strong features and black, lank hair. Kind of attractive in a homely way. He offered a hand.

"Bruce Green. *Boytimes.*"

We shook hands. His grip was warm, firm.

"I just came by to pay my respects." Brown eyes held mine. "Have you changed your mind about talking to me?"

"Man, it must be a slow week for news." I broke off as Chan and Riordan materialized beside us. There was an uneasy pause. Perhaps I looked as tense as I felt. Bruce Green gave my hand a meaningful squeeze before letting it go.

"What are you doing here?" It came out roughly because I was afraid I knew what they were doing there.

Chan said quietly, "Just paying our respects like everyone else, Mr. English."

"This could be viewed as harassment," Bruce Green said.

They stared at me. Stared at Green.

Riordan inquired, "And you are —?"

"Bruce Green. *Boytimes.*"

Their faces said it all.

Green turned to me. "You don't have to talk to them, you know?"

Chan looked pained. Riordan ... well, I momentarily expected a MegaMan reaction of nuclear proportions.

"It's routine, so they tell me."

"I'll be in touch." Green's gaze locked once more with mine.

I nodded. He gave the cops a curt inclination of his head before turning away and vanishing into the line of mourners still filing out through the double doors. He looked too well-groomed, too well-dressed to fit my image of a reporter.

Riordan made a sound of contempt. "Reporters."

Chan said, as though it had just occurred to him, "Mr. English, were you aware that Mr. Hersey had taken out a sizable life insurance policy a few months before he died?"

"No. How sizable?"

"People have committed murder for less," Riordan said.

I was afraid to ask. "Who's the beneficiary?"

Riordan's brows shot up. "Can't you guess?"

I stared at them dumbly. Whatever I said, I knew they would think I was lying. The more I tried to explain, the worse it would look. It was like being in quicksand. The more I struggled, the faster I would sink.

"Excuse me." I pushed past them, following the scattering of mourners down the slope toward the ornamental lake. The ground was soggy from previous days' rain. My shoes squelched in the grass as I made my way to the green canopy positioned a yard from the grave.

I didn't see Bruce Green in the crowd. I was sorry because I had changed my mind about talking to him.

I had changed my mind about a lot of things.

CHAPTER FOUR

Robert's apartment was not sealed. No official yellow tape stretched across the front door proclaiming it a crime scene. As I hesitated on the walkway it seemed to me that it looked like it had always looked. California standard issue white stucco, complete with yellowing palm trees and the soothing rumble of the nearby Hollywood Freeway.

I let myself in using my key. Locking the door behind me, I leaned against it breathing softly, eyes straining in the darkness.

From the other side of the wall came the muffled bawl of heavy metal music, but inside the cold apartment all was silent.

I didn't want to risk turning on the lights. I switched on my pocket flashlight and swung it slowly around the room: your typical West Hollywood studio apartment furnished in early Montgomery Ward. A white sofa bed sat across from an "oak" armoire that doubled as an entertainment center. A Bowflex exercise machine took up half the living room. I glanced over the counter into the kitchenette. There was a sink full of dirty dishes. The apartment smelled stale — worse. I traced the stench to dead flowers in a wine bottle on the counter.

Pressed for time, I crossed to the armoire. Opening the top drawer, I sifted through the undershirts, underpants: several packs of condoms, shirt studs in a leather box, a packet of drugstore prints. I thumbed through the prints quickly. Tara and the kids building snowmen, raking leaves, celebrating a birthday, trimming a Christmas tree. Life without father. I tucked them back between the Lycra leopard bikinis.

It was weird going through Rob's stuff. More painful than I expected. Pretty stupid getting choked up over his sock drawer, I jeered at myself. I wasn't even sure what I was looking for. I raked a latex glove through my hair, wincing as fine hairs pulled.

Rising from my haunches, I moved to the closet. On the upper shelf were two bulging shoe boxes fastened shut with straining rubber bands. When I reached for them a hard and flat object dislodged and fell, whacking me on the head. I swore then waited tensely to see if there was any response to that bump from the apartment next door.

Nothing. The neighbors were probably deaf, judging by the muted thump of drums and bass guitar. I recognized Great White's "What Do You Do for Love."

My flashlight picked out a high school yearbook, loose Christmas cards and a dildo. A dildo in a coat closet?

"For God's sake, Rob!" I muttered, as I had been muttering for years. Like it was Rob's fault he was dead and I was nosing through his personal belongings.

I snatched the dildo up, tucking it deep in the kitchen trash bin, freaking at the idea of Rob's sisters or Tara going through his apartment and finding it. Just who was I trying to protect?

Returning to the living room, I lifted down one of the shoeboxes, folded myself cross-legged on the carpet and removed the lid. Bills, bills and more bills. Paycheck stubs. So many bills. So few paycheck stubs. I wished like hell our last conversation had not been about money.

I finished flipping through the stuffed box admitting that even if there was something there to find I probably wouldn't recognize it. People don't keep bank registers like they used to. There wasn't a lot to make of some loose ATM slips and several returned checks in their envelopes.

I moved on to the next box. Bingo. Letters. Packs of photos. I pulled out the first envelope, recognizing that wild, green ink scrawl. I smoothed out the letter, scanned it quickly. It was signed "Black Beauty."

Talk about your purple prose. *"Sacre bleu,"* I murmured.

I folded the letter up again, stuffed it in the envelope. From outside came a soft brushing sound against the wall.

I went rigid.

There was the scrape of a key in the front door lock. I crunched the lid back on the box and scrambled into the closet, pulling it closed.

Through the wood I heard the front door open and then shut. A band of light appeared beneath the bottom of the closet door. I stared at it in fascination.

A floorboard creaked.

I wondered if Robert's murderer was prowling around on the other side of the door.

In the crowded darkness Robert's clothes brushed against my face, Robert's scent filled my nostrils. It was as though he stood there beside me during any one of the dozens of pranks we'd played as kids. I felt like if I reached out I would brush his hand. I realized I needed to take a piss.

Sweat poured out all over my body as I waited in the stifling darkness. I was surprised the intruder couldn't hear my heart booming away; to me it sounded as loud as if someone were kicking an empty oil drum.

I stiffened as I heard a voice, low. The words were indistinct. Were there two of them? I pressed closer to the door, trying to hear, trying to recognize the voice.

Male. That's all I could tell.

A few more unintelligible words, and then the unmistakable ping of the phone being hung up.

The floor creaked again. The band of light beneath the door vanished. The front door closed as quietly as it had opened. I heard the snick of the lock.

Silence.

I waited quite a while just to be sure.

I expelled a long sigh. Cautiously, I opened the closet and stepped out.

The overhead light switched on. Detective Riordan leaned against the front door, one hand resting casually on his jacket lapel, shoulder holster within easy reach.

"That's one of the oldest tricks in the world, Adrien-with-an-e."

I wasn't sure if he meant his or mine. I stood there breathing in and out in time to the heaving of the beige carpet. From a distance I heard Riordan drawl something else, and then the floor rose up and hit me in the face.

* * * * *

I came to lying on Robert's sofa. Riordan bent over me, sharply, insistently, patting my cheek.

"Rise and shine, Sleeping Beauty. Come on. Open those baby blues. Wake up."

I fluttered my eyelashes. Unglued my mouth. "I'm awake."

Riordan quit patting my cheek. Stared down at me.

"Jesus," I mumbled as the full picture sank in.

"Wrong again." He took my wrist in a cool, professional grip. Looked at his watch for a moment. Grunted.

I watched him passively. I mean, the thing had gone way past humiliation. I couldn't feel much beyond a mild curiosity. Had he been following me? Would he have shot me? And why is it the best looking ones are always straight?

"You know, English, maybe you should consider another line of work. I don't think you're cut out for burglary."

"Are you going to arrest me?" Like I said, it was just mild curiosity. I was too tired to get worked up about it.

His eyes flickered. "I don't know. What are you doing here?"

I pushed up on elbow, fumbled in my breast pocket for my pills, managed to get the cap off. "Could I have a glass of water?"

"You're stalling." But he went into the kitchenette and returned with half a glass of water.

I sort of think if (God forbid) I had HIV or AIDS it would be more acceptable. If you're gay and ill people half expect that anyway. But this ... I can't expect another guy to have patience with it. I don't have patience with it myself.

He regarded me in silence as I sat up gingerly, popped the pills, took the glass and swallowed some water.

"Thanks. How did you know it was me?"

Riordan snorted. "That's your black Ford Bronco parked a block down, isn't it?"

"Oh." I took another swallow and set the glass on the carpet. I raked the hair out of my eyes. My hand was almost steady. I realized he had removed my gloves. I glanced around but didn't see them.

He shook his head. "Listen, Brain Guy, I thought you wrote a book once or something. Didn't it occur to you that we would be watching this place? Don't you think we've gone through all this?" He indicated the shoebox lying where I'd dropped it. "What were you looking for?"

I didn't like to say what had been in my mind: that maybe Rob had tried to blackmail someone. It seemed disloyal, though it was exactly the kind of far-fetched thing he would do.

I said, "Something you missed. Something that would point to who really killed Robert." I met his gaze squarely. "I didn't."

Riordan grinned a crooked grin. "You do know, English, that that is what they all say?"

"I didn't kill him."

He considered me for a long moment with those light, keen eyes. He rubbed his nose thoughtfully. Then he said, "Suppose we go someplace and talk about it?"

* * * * *

We went to Café Noir. Claude greeted us with menus, beaming at what he imagined to be my first date in eight months. I'm not sure if Riordan picked that up but he brusquely excused himself and started for the wash-room, feeling his way through the gloom.

"Oooh la *la,*" twinkled Claude, leading me to an empty booth. "*Très magnifique.*"

"He's a cop," I cut him off. "One of the detectives investigating Robert's murder."

Claude looked aghast. "Why did you bring him *here?*"

His voice rose to a small shriek on the last word.

"Shhhhh," I hissed. "Listen up. They know about the letters."

"They've got them?"

"I saw them in a shoe box at Robert's. Riordan made a point of telling me that they'd already been through all Robert's stuff."

"It was a *trap?*"

I opened my mouth but broke off as the men's room door opened and Riordan stepped out. Claude jerked guiltily up from the table and hastened away toward the kitchen, giving my police escort a wide berth.

A second later Riordan dropped down across from me and said, "So tell me, Jonny Quest, just exactly what were you up to in Hersey's apartment?"

"I already told you. You people have me pegged as the fall guy — or gay."

His dark brows rose. "Excuse me? Have you been arrested? Have you so much as been officially interrogated? Even after I find you breaking and entering —"

"I have a key."

He sucked in a peremptory breath. "Come on, English, I'm trying to be straight with you."

I flicked him a deliberate look under my lashes. "Well, you can see what a waste of time that is."

Our glances held — locked. After a moment Riordan laughed. Short and crisp, but a genuine laugh.

"You're kind of a smart-ass when you're not flat on your face."

Claude returned with gigantic foam-topped mugs of cappuccino. "Decaf for you, *mon petit*," he informed me. He slopped Riordan's in front of him and stalked off. I just hoped he hadn't laced the detective's with strychnine.

I sipped my decaf. I hate decaf.

"While I'm thinking of it, what's the name of your doctor?" Riordan took out a notebook and pen.

"Why?"

"Why do you think?"

I gave him the name of my doctor and he put the notepad away. That was a relief. I didn't know if I was up to another interrogation right then.

I said, "There's such a thing as patient-doctor confidentiality."

"Relevant medical records can be subpoenaed. A doctor is not a priest. Besides, this might work to your advantage. You never know." He rubbed the back of his neck, his restless gaze wandering over the other tables, the other customers. I deduced he was uncomfortable lest he be mistaken for one of my kindred. He needn't have worried. Café Noir was not a "gay" restaurant, whatever that is.

"Have you found whoever it was that Robert was meeting that night?"

"We have only your word that Robert left to meet someone else. He went back to the Blue Parrot looking for you."

I put my cup down with a bang. "Tell me this. Do you have any other suspects or am I it?"

"You know I can't tell you that."

"I'm not asking you to name names. Are you considering the possibility that I *didn't* kill Robert?"

His face hardened. "Hell yes. If we weren't, you'd be wearing orange PJs right now."

Not exactly words of comfort but I relaxed a fraction. If he planned to arrest me we'd be going directly to jail, not sipping cappuccino like civilized folk. For some reason I had been granted a reprieve. Why? Because the cops' grounder case wasn't such a ground ball after all? Riordan felt around in his pocket and then set something small and white on the granite table between us. I felt him observing me for any change of expression.

"What is it?"

"You don't know?"

"I know it's a chess piece."

"You play chess?"

I answered warily, "Yeah."

"What piece is this?"

I picked it up. "Queen." It was one of those cheap pressed plastic pieces. Nothing unique or memorable about it.

"You and Robert played chess?"

"When we were kids. I haven't played in years."

"Why's that?"

I shrugged, replaced the piece on the table top. "I don't know. No one to play with."

"Boo hoo."

I re-revised my original opinion. Riordan was indeed an asshole. But he was probably pretty good at reading people — and manipulating them.

He added, "A piece exactly like this was found on Hersey's body."

"On his body?"

"Clutched in his hand." Riordan studied me, and a weird half-smile curved his lips. "As Hersey lay dying, his assailant pressed this into his hand and folded his fingers around it. Held it closed. There were bruises on Hersey's hand."

"Fingerprints?"

"No fingerprints."

I swallowed hard. Riordan reached across and pocketed the game piece. "Keep that to yourself. We haven't released it to the press yet."

"Why tell me?"

I couldn't read the expression on his face. "Because I think you know what this chess piece means."

I shook my head. "No. Unless the reference is to a queen. To Robert's being gay."

"That's one explanation obviously."

"I don't have another."

Riordan sipped his cappuccino. He did not look like a cappuccino kind of guy. "You think about it, Adrien-with-an-e. I bet it comes to you."

* * * * *

The first Saturday of each month meant brunch with She Who Must Be Placated.

Lisa, my mother, has never forgiven me for a number of things, but being gay is not one of them. My main offense was my decision at age twenty-five that I was well enough to live outside the parental holdings. Worse, to start a "grubby little shop" on the money left to me by my paternal grandmother. As Lisa has no interest in my life as an autonomous adult, our brunches make for rather superficial conversation. Yet neither of us quite likes to give up this delicate tradition of chitchat over blueberry cream cheese blintzes and pots of Earl Grey tea.

Today, the weather being sunny, we brunched on the terrace overlooking the scrubby green hills of Porter Ranch. The February breeze whipped the white linen and scattered *Sombreuil* rose petals from the garden into the blueberry sauce. Lisa, still trim as a dancer in an Aran knit sweater and lavender leggings, was pouring tea into fragile china cups as I stepped through the French doors.

"I was beginning to think you weren't coming, darling. What do you think of my hair?" she invited as I kissed her cheek.

"You look like Audrey Hepburn's little sister."

"Liar." She preened.

I steadied the table as a gust of wind rocked it. The china rattled in genteel protest. "Maybe we should do this inside."

"Why? I love this weather. It's very nearly spring. The daffodils are out."

"So is a hurricane advisory." But I sat down across from her, shook out my napkin — barely kept it from blowing away.

Lisa placed a cup in front of me. "And how are you darling? You look tired. You're not overdoing again?"

"No. I'm fine."

"You know what the doctors said."

"Mm. How was the SPCA Ball?'

Lisa sat back and laughed her pretty silvery laugh. "Darling, it was a fiasco! You'd have laughed yourself sick. You *must* come next year, now promise, Adrien!"

"We'll see."

"You always say that." She pouted briefly. She's the sort of woman who looks delightful pouting — of which she is well aware. "It would do you good to get out. To meet people. To have fun."

She was probably right about that, but somehow I didn't think hanging out with a bunch of cat-crazy geezers was going to cure what ailed me.

I murmured noncommittally and picked up the gold-edged pink tea cup. The handle was too small to actually get my fingers through. I always felt like I was playing house at these brunches. All that was missing was a giant imaginary friend. I could have used a friend here.

Leaning forward, her violet eyes brimming with a melting tenderness, she said earnestly, "I know Mel hurt you terribly when he left."

Oh God. "Lisa, really …"

She sat bolt upright. "Darling! I'd nearly forgotten. I have some *awful* news."

I waited, my gaze wandering over the manicured lawn, the pool glittering in the sunshine, the apricot and coral rose bushes trembling in the wind.

"You remember that little friend of yours from high school? Oh what *was* his name? Well, he's *dead*."

"I know."

Her eyes went wide like a startled fawn. "How can you know? I only heard from Jane Quinn this morning and she'd only talked to Annette Penick last night."

I'd forgotten the maternal communication system, even more complex and infallible than Holmes's Baker Street Irregulars.

"He worked for me, Lisa," I reminded her patiently.

"Worked for you? When?"

"Up until he … died."

"In Buffalo?"

"You're thinking of Sioux City."

"I am? I'm sure Jane said Buffalo."

"It was Sioux City, but he's been living in West Hollywood for the past nine months."

My mother bit her lip, looking adorably perplexed. "Darling, what *are* you babbling about? This happened a couple of months ago — and he died in Buffalo. Oh, Adrien, you'll never believe! At least … " She paused, looking troubled. "Darling, *you* don't wear dresses, do you?"

I choked on my Earl Grey. "I'm not a transvestite, no. Neither was Robert."

"Who?"

"Robert Hersey. The friend who died."

"Robert Hersey is *dead?*" Her tea cup hit the saucer with a clatter. She gaped at me. "Darling, *when?* That's horrific. Why, you were *such* chums. Whatever happened? Not ... ." Her voice sank. *"AIDS?"*

Sidetracked, I tried to explain, leaving out the awful parts, which didn't leave much to say. Lisa was appalled and wanted to know all the awful parts. I did manage to avoid telling her I was the police's favorite suspect, but with all the hedging it took awhile before I remembered the original point of our conversation.

"Lisa, you said another friend of mine had died?"

She hit mental rewind and her eyes grew saucer-like once more. "Oh! Yes. In Buffalo." She gazed at me sympathetically. "I shouldn't laugh because it's really quite *tragic*. What if it was suicide? Think of his poor mother. It's just that it's *so* undignified. And what a spooky coincidence! Skippy or Corky or Whatever-His-Name was Corday fell out the window of some posh hotel. Twelve stories down in a polka dot cocktail frock and white pumps. *White* pumps, darling, and that was *weeks* past Labor Day!"

CHAPTER FIVE

"The police were here," Angus informed me when I got back to the shop that afternoon.

My heart sank. "Again? Why? What did they want?"

Angus mumbled something. I snapped nervously, *"What?* Can't you speak up?"

"There was just one of them this time. A Detective Regan, I think."

"Shit. What does he want *now*?" This was merely a rhetorical whine because Angus clearly had no idea.

"Well, is he coming back? Am I supposed to call him?" *Is there a warrant out for my arrest?*

Angus shrugged. Not really his problem. His problem was those tiny agitated twins of me mirrored in the lens of his glasses.

I headed upstairs and Angus called softly, "Some flowers came for you."

The flowers lay outside the door to my flat in one of those long white florist boxes.

I don't get many flowers. In fact, I don't know if I've ever gotten flowers. I pulled the lid off and gawked. Black hollyhocks and a dozen blood-red roses, perfect to the last thorn — which pricked my thumb. I sucked on my thumb and gingerly lifted out the card.

Nothing to him falls early, or too late ...

No signature.

For one crazy moment the thought flitted through my brain that Riordan had left them. Don't ask me why. He didn't look like a hearts and flowers kind of guy, not even for his best gal (of whom, I'm sure, he had many).

The roses were beautiful and no doubt expensive, but as I beheld them, nestled in their silvery tissue, I felt the hairs on the back of my neck rise. Something about the black hollyhocks and the black satin ribbon looked funereal. And a handwritten unsigned card? Was that romantic or plain old sinister?

Goin' to the chapel and I'm gonna get buried?

I tried to think of someone who might send me flowers. Anyone. I couldn't think of a single person I was on flowery terms with — let alone flowers with cryptic notes.

Downstairs the cash register rang; I heard the rustle of paper and Angus thanking a customer for their business. I heard the shop bell jingle.

A simple explanation occurred: a screw-up at the florist's. Flowers meant for Robert's funeral had been sent in care of me.

Of course. It made perfect sense. What else could it be?

But even while I assured myself that this was the only plausible explanation, I felt uneasy. Because if it wasn't a screw-up and the roses weren't from anyone I knew ...?

Nah. Too far-fetched.

Unlocking the door to my flat, I carried the box inside and dropped the roses in the trash bin. I don't care that much about flowers, really. And these were a little too elegiac.

Or maybe I was getting superstitious in my old age. First Robert's murder, and now this gruesome coincidence of Rusty — Richard Corday — dying in Buffalo.

Rusty. I hadn't thought of him in years. He was the first of our clique to come out — and what a misery his adolescent life had become. I hoped like hell he hadn't jumped. I hoped like hell the last fifteen years of his life had been happier than the first.

There was a small sound behind me. I whirled to find Angus standing in the doorway to my kitchen.

"Jesus Christ! What are you *doing?"*

No doubt he heard the fright in my voice. No doubt people on the street did. He raised his hands apologetically. "Sorry, man," he said quietly. "I forgot to tell you. Your friend's been calling all day."

"What friend?"

"Mr. La Pierra."

Claude. I relaxed. "Right. Thanks."

He continued to regard me. Then he looked at the box of flowers in the trash. He looked back at me.

"Hay fever," I offered. "The antihistamines make me jittery." I smiled tentatively but Angus did not respond. He nodded and edged out of the kitchen as though afraid to turn his back on me.

I locked the door after him and sat down to call Claude.

"Where the hell have you been?" Claude greeted me, sounding less French Quarter and more South Central than usual. "You led them straight to me, you — you — *imbecile!*"

"What are you talking about?"

"The one! The cops! They were *here. Here* in my *restaurant.*" He made it sound like the Huns were marching on Paris.

"I told you they had your letters. How long did you think it would take to put a name to 'Black Beauty'?"

There was a silence filled by the background noise of voices and clanging pots and pans, and then Claude said spitefully, "Ha! And as to that, *ma belle,* he was asking as much about you as me, your blue knight in shining Armor All."

"Who? Detective Riordan? What do you mean? What kinds of things was he asking?"

"*Personal* things!" shrieked Claude. "Who, what, where, when, and how often! I don't trust him, that cop. He's up to something."

I bit back a flare of panic and said, "It's normal procedure, right? They have to check up on everybody who knew Robert."

Claude made a sound that in English translates to "Paugh!" "There's something about that dick. Dick — that's the operative word. Yeah, I know him from somewhere. ..."

He brooded without speaking for a moment. I wondered if the cops were tapping either or both of our phones?

"Claude, who was Robert seeing? Who did he go to meet that night?"

He put his hand over the mouthpiece and yelled unintelligibly before returning to the line to say in a surly voice, "How should I know?"

"You know," I coaxed. "You always know."

"People tell me things," Claude admitted grudgingly. "I hear things."

"He had started seeing someone, hadn't he?"

"Some*one*? He wasn't a one-man woman, Adrien. He was a *slut*."

The bitterness in Claude's voice took me aback. Had it been serious on Claude's side?

I persisted slowly, "Robert left in the middle of an argument with me to go meet someone. Someone he couldn't — or wouldn't — put off."

Claude's laugh was shrill. "And he winds up doing the Ginsu with a trick in an alley. It slices, it dices, and *that's not all*."

For a second I wasn't sure what Claude meant. Was he joking or was there an underlying message? Did he know about the chess piece Robert's killer had left?

I said, "Was Robert with a trick? Or was *he* hustling?"

"Suddenly I'm the expert? The girl liked to fuck, *mon ange*. He wasn't particular."

"He needed money. Was he tricking?"

"I don't know."

"You said he was with a trick. Why? You must have had some reason."

Silence.

"Stay out of it, Adrien. Let the cops handle it," Claude said finally.

"You just said you don't trust the cops."

"I know what I said. Better jail, than dead. *N'est-ce pas?*"

I opened my mouth but the phone disconnected. Slowly I replaced the receiver.

I sat there staring at my grandmother's violet sprig-pattern china gleaming behind the cupboard windows. A trick, Claude said. I didn't think so. It didn't fit with Robert's mood in the days before his death. He had been happy — hell, *gay*. And secretive.

Robert loved secrets. His own and other people's. And he wasn't above dropping hints. It amused him to watch people sweat. That was one reason

I thought he might take it a step further (admittedly a big step) and offer to exchange silence for money. The trouble was I couldn't imagine Rob privy to any information worth paying for — let alone worth killing for. Homosexuality just wasn't what it used to be in the Golden Age of mystery writing.

Why had he come back to the Blue Parrot that night?

Would it have changed anything if I had still been waiting?

Why had he come back? Had his date bailed? Had they argued? Or had Robert changed his mind before he ever got there?

Why hadn't he come back to the shop if he wanted to talk to me?

I realized that I would never know what Robert had wanted to tell me.

Depressed, I went into the bedroom, lost the Hugo Boss blazer and the kicks, changed into black sweats. Catching a glimpse of myself in the mirror I thought, *if you died tomorrow who would grieve for you?*

Whatever Robert had been and done, he had people to grieve for him. Not just the usual suspects, but children. Hell, even an ex-wife.

Tara had caught me up as I was leaving the funeral.

She avoided my eyes, scraping a grass divot from her high heel. "Adrien, look — I apologize. I shouldn't have said all that. I'd been drinking. I never could handle it."

After a moment I said, "Sure. You were upset. I understand."

"It was just a phase Bob was going through. He was upset about a lot of things. But he still loved me. He told me that the last time we talked. I know we would have worked it out eventually. I shouldn't have taken it out on you. You were a good friend in your way."

"Forget it, Tara."

She looked up then, her hands fluttering helplessly as though she wanted to make a gesture but didn't know how. I moved to hug her. Dodged her hat. We embraced awkwardly, stepped back. I looked at the kids: Rob's kids. The boy, Bobby Jr., was one of those golden-curled adorable tykes.

Holding his hand was a cherub-like little girl, equally golden-curled and rose-lipped. I could never remember her name. Twin pairs of green eyes gazed up at me. Rob's eyes gazing at me. I felt unutterably sad. I wanted to do something for them.

"Tara, is there anything —?"

She shook her head quickly. "It's sweet of you, Adrien, but no. There's nothing. Not now." Behind the veil her pale eyes were unwavering and tearless.

I had never understood her. Never understood what Rob saw in her. Even back in high school she had been a total mystery to me. Granted, all girls had been a mystery — and pretty much still were.

Remembering the adolescent Tara reminded me of Rusty.

I dragged out the storage trunk in the spare room and began rummaging through it: photo albums, letters from Mel (why did I keep this stuff?), half-finished manuscripts, college magazines, and finally, at the bottom of the chest, my high school yearbook. Gold script on blue vinyl lettered out: *West Valley Academy.* "West End" the public school kids called it.

I wasn't sure what I was searching for as I glanced over the faded inscriptions, trite then, but sort of poignant now. *Good luck in college. Let's stay friends 4-ever. Luv, Brooke.* Who the hell was Brooke? What had happened to all these "Friends 4-ever?" Mostly I recalled my senior year as a panicked struggle to catch up while my mother and her Greek chorus of doctors waited in the wings for my anticipated collapse.

Memories wafted out of those glossy black and white pages like the scent of formaldehyde in biology class. I studied a photo of Rob. This was one of those carefully staged candid shots taken in the journalism club. Tara stood in the background watching Rob pretend to load film in his camera. I shut the yearbook with a snap and went downstairs.

"If you want to take the rest of the day, go ahead," I told Angus.

He shrugged. "I don't mind if you want to work in the back. It's pretty dead."

I must have winced because he whispered, "Sorry."

I looked at the book he was reading: *The Encyclopedia of Demonology.*

Catching my gaze, Angus muttered, "It's for my thesis."

The hell you say. I opened my mouth, decided I didn't really want to know, and went into my office. Sitting at the desk, I thumbed through the mail for the past week. It all seemed to be addressed to someone else. Someone who gave a damn.

The phone rang next to my elbow. I ignored it. It stopped ringing abruptly.

"Phone call for you," Angus yelled from the store floor, and I nearly fell out of my chair. The good news was that there was nothing permanently wrong with his vocal cords. Though we probably needed to work on his phone skills.

I picked up.

Silence.

"Can I help you?"

Click. Dial tone.

I shrugged. Hung up.

So what was my next move? Robert was dead and the police thought I had killed him. At the very least they were convinced I knew something about his death.

Maybe the police would figure it all out. That's what they did for a living, right? Stranger things had happened.

Still, it couldn't hurt to be a bit proactive here. Detective Riordan believed I knew more than I thought I did — assuming that whole tête-à-tête hadn't been some kind of trap.

I opened a drawer and pulled out a pad of legal paper. *Great. Good start.* I picked up a pen, neatly numbered one through ten. *Okay. First thing ...*

I eyed the blank page. Just in time I stopped myself from writing DO LAUNDRY.

Focus.

After a moment I drew a chess piece. A pawn. Was that Freudian or Jungian or plain doodling? Where the hell did one begin? Who would want to kill Robert? Tara? Claude? It was preposterous. Yet someone *had* murdered him.

Most murders are not committed by strangers. But I couldn't help coming back to the theory of a random act of violence. Someone who hated gays in general? Someone who left a "queen" as a calling card? Maybe even a serial killer. Although in that case where was the series of victims?

The police were investigating Robert's death as an isolated event — and me as the prime suspect.

Or were they?

What had Riordan been up to showing me that chess piece? Was I supposed to betray myself with my sinister knowledge of advances, gambits, jeopardy and end game? Was I supposed to turn white as the plastic queen and confess all?

Or did he really want my help?

That evening I was watching *Frenchman's Creek* — is it just me or does Basil Rathbone look hot in that long curled wig? — eating a bowl of Apple Crunch Muselix when Riordan returned.

He was on his own, wearing Levi's and a white Henley, and looking good enough to eat.

"I take it this isn't a social call," I said as he followed me up the stairs to my flat. "I won't offer you a beer."

"You can offer me a beer," he said. He leaned against the kitchen counter studying the grape leaf stencil border on the opposite wall. He crowded my kitchen — and it was a large kitchen. He made me self-conscious, which was annoying as hell.

I got a couple of Harp beers and earned the first flicker of approval I had seen from the man. Our fingers brushed exchanging the frosty bottle. There was a snap of static electricity. I'm surprised it wasn't spontaneous combustion.

"Can I sit?" Riordan indicated the table.

"Sure. Where are my manners? I was just waiting for you to arrest me."

He shot me a sardonic look and sat down, tilting the chair back on its legs.

"So what have you got for me?"

"I … beg your pardon?" I think I actually blushed, that's the direction my thoughts were going.

Riordan's dark brows shot up in that supercilious way. "You're supposed to be helping save your sorry ass by figuring out the connection between Hersey and that chess piece. Remember?"

"I told you what I thought it meant." I leaned against the fridge. I felt safer on my feet when I was around him.

"That's it? Queen? You think we're facing some chess-playing fag-hating Mr. Stranger Danger?"

I shrugged. "What do you want? The history of chess? It's a game of intellect played between two people. Each player has sixteen pieces. So if you're dealing with a serial killer maybe he plans on killing sixteen people. Or sixty-four. There are sixty-four squares on a game board."

"We're not dealing with a serial killer."

"How do you know? Maybe Robert was the first."

"I know." He took a swig of beer. Looked me over. "How tall are you? Five ten? Five eleven?"

"Six feet."

"In your dreams."

Five foot eleven and a half actually, but I wasn't going to argue the point.

"Hersey was what, five nine? Short but built. Worked out regularly. Anyway, the ME's findings indicate his assailant was probably four to five inches taller. You could have done it, but you'd have had to stand on your tippy toes."

We both stared at my feet in their white crew socks. I curled and uncurled my toes nervously.

"I think you'd have had trouble hoisting the body into the trash bin." Riordan added, "I had a talk with your doctor, by the way. He says your overall health is good, although you work too hard and drink too much caffeine. If I understood him correctly your main trouble is an irregular heartbeat."

"I had rheumatic fever as a kid. The valves of my heart are damaged."

"Yeah, so he said. But he said normal physical exertion isn't so much the problem for you as sudden shocks. You don't react well to surprises; that I've seen."

"He didn't rule out the possibility of my stabbing someone to death," I concluded.

Riordan smiled that crooked smile. "He said it would be a strain, but he didn't rule it out; no."

That meant zero. Lisa had a string of doctors who could testify I was practically an invalid. "Isn't it true that for every expert witness the prosecution presents, the defense can find an equally credible witness to challenge?"

"Sure. But we're not going to trial, English. We're trying to find out who actually killed your old — er — pal. See, I'd just as soon arrest the right perp to start with. Saves the taxpayers money."

"How noble." I drank from my beer. Beer and Muselix. It's what's for supper.

"Hey, you may find this hard to grasp, but I believe in the system. It works, so long as everybody does their job."

I said dryly, "You're going to tell me cops never make a mistake?"

"Not as often as the movies would like you to think. Our legal system may not be perfect, but it's a hell of a lot better than anything else going."

I met his eyes briefly, considered those rough, masculine good looks, considered a nose that had obviously been broken more than once — and no wonder.

"Robert owed a lot of people money — including me."

"You think one of Hersey's creditors called in his loan? Not a very profitable way to do business."

I set my beer aside, turned, rinsed out my cereal bowl. I turned off the water. Through the sink window the moon hung in the night smog looking old and tarnished. From the other room Basil in the role of Lord Rockingham was purring threats in that wicked public school accent, filling the silence between us.

Riordan said idly, "Chan thinks you killed Hersey. Chan has pretty good instincts."

"So arrest me."

"I would if we had enough to convict. Right now I don't need the ACLU breathing down my neck."

I turned to face him, asked flat out, "Do *you* think I murdered Robert?"

Riordan shrugged. "I've been wrong before. Not often." He scraped at the label on the beer bottle with his thumbnail. "For the record, you're right about the money angle. Hersey owed big time. Credit cards, child support and some of the less — conventional — money stores."

"Loan sharks?"

His lips twitched at my tone. "Uh huh. We are pursuing that angle."

"But you don't think maybe some street thug —?"

"Like I said, it's not a profitable way to do business. You generally don't start by killing the borrower. First you loosen a few teeth. Break a few bones."

I got Riordan a second beer. He didn't seem to notice. No doubt used to being waited on hand and foot by doting females.

"I've been thinking," I said slowly. "Robert was seeing someone. Not just a pickup stick. There were flowers in his apartment. Roses. Hustlers don't bring you flowers. Rob wasn't the kind to buy himself flowers. Find the guy Robert went to meet that night and I think you'll nail whoever killed him."

"Unfortunately there was no card," Riordan pointed out. So much for thinking the police might have missed this. "*You* could have sent Hersey those flowers for all we know."

That reminded me. I pushed away from the counter, pulled the box of flowers out of the trash and threw them on the table.

"Gee, this is so sudden," he drawled.

I ignored him. "These arrived today. There's a card somewhere." I returned to the trash bin, rifling around 'til I found the card between the empty cans of Tab and frozen food boxes. I slid the paper rectangle across the table to Riordan. "I tried to tell myself there was a mix-up at the florist's."

He picked it up. Read it. Shrugged. "You could have sent these to yourself."

"You could at least go to the florist and find out."

"What am I finding out? You want me to believe there's a connection here?"

"I don't know. I just have a feeling. …"

"Feminine intuition?"

"Fuck you!"

Riordan pushed his chair further back, precariously balanced, as immune to civility as he was to gravity. "Temper, temper." He raised those reckless brows. "Ready to start reaching for the kitchen knives?"

"I think you've already checked out the cutlery."

He grinned, unperturbed. "Yeah?"

"Yeah. Monday, when you pretended to be looking for prowlers in my closet."

He laughed. "Hey, it's not much of a closet is it?"

"No. It's not. I don't like closets. Life's too short to spend hiding in the dark."

He stuck the florist's card in his shirt pocket and said, "Tell you what. I'll check out this flower shop. You do me a favor. Tell me about Claude La Pierra."

"Great. Now you want me to rat out my friends."

"If he killed Hersey, he's no friend. Are you and La Pierra lovers?"

"No." I must have shown my surprise.

Riordan said, "You took a helluva chance going after those letters. That is what you were after in Hersey's pad, wasn't it?"

"I told you why I went there."

"Uh huh. And then you suggested we swing by La Pierra's so you could warn him we'd already found them." He laughed at my expression. "You've got balls, English. I'll give you that."

"Look, Claude's one of the kindest, most generous —"

"Blah, blah, blah. Did you know La Pierra a.k.a. Humphrey Washington has a juvenile arrest sheet as long as your arm?"

That stopped me cold. It took a moment to recall my argument. "I thought juvenile records weren't admissible?"

"Like I said, nobody's on trial yet. I'm just telling you that homeboy has done time for assault with a deadly weapon. He carved his initials in a play-mate's buttocks."

For some reason I wanted to ask, which pair of initials? The ones he was born with or the set he chose? Instead I said, "People change, right? That's the point of prison."

"Not always. That's the point of the death penalty."

His face was hard. Not a guy with much sympathy for weakness. I said, "People grow up."

Riordan rolled his eyes. "Did you happen to read any of what he wrote your friend Hersey? And I quote, 'To say goodbye to the thing that was peeled back and pulpy like a grape. And I press my mouth and unpeel your moans, and my tongue flicks out switch blade fox red tongue, and I kill the thing I love. Love the thing I kill.'"

I blinked. "Okay. So he's not Robert Frost."

"Or how about this gem? 'Harvest in the midnight of your body, betrayed and fucked by a smile you practice in the bath of your urinal. I carve the entrails from your ego, bleating bleeding mouth.' "

"The scariest part is you memorized this stuff."

"No, the scariest part is what Hersey looked like when La Pierra, or someone who thinks like him, got finished."

I swallowed hard. "Bad poetry is not a crime. Not that you can prosecute anyway. I don't think you understand the — um — creative temperament. A guy like Claude gets the violence out of his system by writing."

"And what lovely writing he has — depending on the medium."

CHAPTER SIX

Bad dreams. That's one of the downsides of living alone: waking in the middle of the night with no one to reach for. No warm sleeping body to snuggle against. No reassuring snores from beside you. Nothing but queen-size 500-thread cotton percale solitude.

I don't remember what I dreamed, but I woke drenched in sweat, my heart banging away like a broken shutter. It took a moment or two to realize where I was; that the tangle of sheets was all that held me prisoner, that the threatening rumble was only rain drumming on the roof, gurgling in the rain gutters.

I sat up, switched on the bedside lamp. The light from the pink glass shade was soft and mellow, illuminating the heavy walnut furniture I'd inherited from my Grandmother Anna's Sonora horse ranch.

My grandmother was a kind of family legend. Back in the '30s when divorce was still a scandal, she had left her husband and gone off to breed horses in what was, in those days, desolate country. She wore pants, smoked cigarettes, and could throw a lasso and shoot a rifle like Annie Oakley. I used to spend summers there, to the chagrin of my mother, tied to her husband's family by the purse strings. When I was eight my grandmother died and left her money to me. The ranch was mine too, but I had never been back.

This bedroom suite had been her own: no Bombay Company knock-offs; the four-poster bed and clawfoot dresser with green marble top were built back in the days when one's furnishings outlasted generations of one's family — and in this case a couple of world wars. Vintage books, old china, antiques; maybe I love old things so much because I feel impermanent myself.

I shook out the blankets and sheets, punched up the pillows. The clock said 2:02 a.m. The street lamps outside the rain-starred windows glowed dimly. It was very quiet. This mostly commercial part of the city was like a ghost town after business hours. I lay back and tried to convince myself I could go back to sleep.

As Riordan would say, uh huh.

When I was younger I used to lie awake listening to my heartbeat, breaking into a sweat when it seemed to skip or double beat. Fortunately I've got over that, developing what Mel called a "healthy fatalism."

A hot drink would be nice, I thought. But the idea of cold wooden floors and the dark beyond my locked bedroom door was discouraging.

To distract myself I started mentally blue-penciling the sequel to *Murder Will Out*. I realized I was increasingly dissatisfied with my series protagonist, Jason Leland. I wished now I had made him bigger and blonder and a little rougher around the edges.

That was when the phone rang.

The shrill of bells went through my nervous system like an electric shock. After a second I hung over the side of the bed, fishing underneath for the phone. I found it, knocked the receiver off, found it again and dragged the phone out.

"Hello?" I rasped.

Silence.

No, not silence. The line was live, and faintly I could hear breathing.

I opened my mouth. Then I closed it. I waited.

I could hear him — her? — breathing.

How long? A few seconds? A minute? It felt like forever before, eerily, the person on the other end giggled and hung up.

I finally fell asleep with the phone off the hook and the lights blazing.

Sunday passed without incident.

I called a few of Robert's friends, trying to get a lead on who he had been seeing. *Nada*. If Rob had been involved, it must have only been very recently. I knew he would not have confided in his family, who still refused to believe he was gay.

On Monday I called the West Hollywood office of *Boytimes* and was informed they had never heard of Bruce Green.

I was still chewing over that one when Tara showed up with the kids. As usual they looked like a picture out of *Family Circle*. Perfectly groomed and color-coordinated.

"I want to apologize again for the things I said to you on the phone. I don't know why I said them," she said.

There was an awkward pause while we both considered why she had said them. Before I could respond she added, "We're flying back to Sioux City tomorrow. Before I go I wanted to give you this. It was Bob's. It must have meant something to him. He asked me to send it to him a few weeks ago."

She handed me the book she had under her arm.

I took the yearbook , examined gold print on blue. *West Valley Academy.*

"These are your memories too, Tara."

"No. This was Bob's junior year. My family didn't move to California until that following summer. You were still in the hospital."

"That's right. I'd forgotten."

"All Bob's friends forget that." She smiled oddly. "I used to think it was because I fit in so well; like I'd always been part of the group. Now I realize it was because I made so little impression on his friends. In his life."

"That's not true."

"Of course it is," she said impatiently.

The girl, Hannah, pointed at the Tab I held and said, "Coke. Want." Bobby Jr. nudged her in warning.

Relieved at this interruption I fled upstairs, grabbed a couple of Cokes, brought them down and handed them out. Tara looked slightly exasperated but set about popping tops and mopping the instantaneous spills off her pristine children and my hardwood floor.

When she got back to her feet, she said deliberately, "The fact is I was always a little jealous of you, Adrien. Even before I really knew about you. Sometimes I think that if you hadn't gone off to Stanford, Bob wouldn't have married me."

"Rob never did anything he didn't want to."

Was that supposed to cheer her up? She wasn't dumb. She knew what I wasn't saying.

Tara said, "A couple of years at JC. The job at IBM. Then the move to Iowa. He couldn't settle into anything."

"He couldn't settle here either."

She glared at me for a moment, then some of the rigidity left her face. "Thank you for saying that." She seemed to be looking past me into the distance. "It's so *weird*. I remember when I transferred into West Valley. Bob seemed so — so — *together*. I could never have imagined how it would all turn out. Everyone liked him. He was on the tennis team and the school paper. He belonged to all those clubs. Really, he barely had time for me, but I still loved being with him. Well, he wrote me songs, poems. That was part of it: he was different from other boys."

This is the point where Riordan would have snickered.

I said, "He was a good friend."

She smiled that funny smile. "You would say that. I remember how he was always taking off to see his sick friend. The rich kid with the heart condition. And I liked that about him. I thought that showed the kind of person he was."

"That *was* the kind of person he was," I said. "Rob was the only guy who came to see me in the hospital. When I got home he used to bring my classwork over, library books, whatever I needed. He used to sit there and talk about the tennis tournaments and who was boffing who, and Mrs. Lechter's wig falling off in biology."

Those were things I hadn't thought about in a long time. Remembering them, I thought that maybe that was one reason, despite all that had come later, that I had never stopped loving him. When I had been sick and scared and lonely he had been there with the dirty jokes and the Tears for Fears CDs.

Her gaze zeroed in on mine. "Did he talk about me?"

I hesitated. "I don't remember most of it. It was a long time ago."

Tara said shortly, "He didn't talk about you either. He cut classes, he forgot our dates, but he never missed going over to your house. You two must have been laughing behind my back the whole time."

"No, we weren't. I didn't even know about —" I thought better of that. "We didn't even realize we were — we didn't admit it anyway."

"I guess it should have occurred to me. Just the fact that he never pushed for more. My God, I was naïve!"

Well, she was past the denial stage. Maybe it was a good thing.

I said, "Tara, I'm not sure what you want. Why are you belittling what you two shared? He married you, you had a family together. Robert had a lot of problems. I don't know that they even had anything to do with his being gay."

She flinched at the word. Looked automatically to the kids. Hannah was dribbling Coke down her pink overalls. Bobby Jr. stared at me with those tilted green eyes that reminded me of Robert.

Her laugh was brittle. "You must be a terrible writer. You always want a happy ending. Well, there isn't one. I can't forgive him." For a moment tears glittered in her eyes. She blinked them away. "At least ... I've been talking to my therapist." She drew a deep breath. "We've agreed that I need to move on. To let go. That's why I'm here. To close this chapter. To do that I have to set it right with you."

Closure. Who couldn't understand that? But I wasn't the one she needed to make peace with; I was just the only one available.

We hugged, another one of those minimal body contact embraces. I realized it was probably the last time I would see her or the kids.

"Let me know how you get on, Tara," I urged.

She smiled, made some vague reply. I understood that I was just something else she wanted to close the book on.

On her way out, kids in tow, Tara paused and wrinkled her nose. "You know, Adrien, you might want to check for mice."

* * * * *

At noon Angus asked if he could take the rest of the day off. As still as he was, the shop seemed uncannily empty without him. Every creak, every rustle had me looking over my shoulder.

The phone rang twice. Hang-ups both times.

Around three in the afternoon I poured boiling water into one of those Styrofoam cups of Nissin noodles for a late lunch. By then the shop was busy again, and when Claude called I was in the middle of adding up credit for two boxes of 1960s paperbacks coated in layers of nostalgic dust that had me sneezing my head off.

"Can you talk?" Claude demanded.

"No, I'll have to call you back."

"Listen, I remember where I know him from!"

"Know who?" I tried to cradle the phone between my shoulder and cheek while I continued calculating.

Claude mumbled something I assumed was gutter French ending in, "— dick-head!"

"Are you addressing me?"

"*Oui.* I'm addressing you about that dick-head, Reargun, or whatever his name is. The dude's a freaking faggot. He's as queer as a Susan B. Anthony dollar. He's —"

The phone slipped off my shoulder. I lost my place on the calculator. Accidentally hit "clear" instead of "total." "What are you talking about?"

"I saw him, *cherie*, last night at Ball and Chain."

"What's Ball and Chain?"

"*Morbleu*, I forget the sheltered life you lead. Ball and Chain is a leather club."

"*Qu'est-ce que c'est?*" I said faintly.

"*Vous m'avez entendu, bébé.* Guys in black leather. Handcuffs and chains."

The kind of thing Robert toyed with.

"He was probably undercover or something."

"No! You're not listening to me. I've seen him there before. He's a *member*. He's a *master.*"

"He's a —" I couldn't finish the thought, let alone the sentence. My mind literally boggled at the idea of Riordan decked out in black leather. Riordan in a biker cap. Riordan in black leather pants. Was some guy wearing Riordan's collar right now? Was some guy wearing Riordan's marks on his ass right now? It seemed comical, ludicrous.

Then I got another mental image of him, broad chest covered in blond pelt, muscular forearms, big smooth cock jutting out of a silky nest. Riordan ordering me down on my knees, his hand tangling in my hair as he pulled my head toward his heat. The laugh died in my throat.

Claude was running on, jubilant at "catching *le grand gros porc* out."

I interrupted. "Claude, shut up for a second. Are you sure?"

"Of course I'm sure! I *told* you I recognized him. I *told* you I didn't trust him. Well, doesn't *this* simply change everything!"

"What does it change?"

"Everything. I'm going to have it out with him. I'm going to warn him that if he doesn't back off maybe his pals downtown would like to know about Detective Reargun's extracurricular activities."

"Holy Hell!" I caught the face of the woman who stood at the counter, a stack of The Cat Who books in hand. I turned away, lowering my voice. "Are you *nuts*? You're going to threaten a cop?"

"Not any old copper," cooed Claude. "Mr. Tie-You-Up-And-Beat-The-Shit-Out-Of-You-Before-I-Shoot-My-Load-Up-Your-Ass *Detective* Reargun."

I closed my eyes, the better to focus — or maybe to hide my eyes from the launch of Claude's Hindenburg. "Let me get this straight. Are you *trying* to get arrested? Even if you're right, Riordan won't stand down. You'll only make him determined to nail *you*. Jesus, you'll be lucky if he doesn't find an excuse for blowing your head off."

"We'll see."

I couldn't believe Claude was this dim. Riordan was not the right temperament for a blackmail victim. Even I could see that. Although he apparently engaged in activities that made him a prime target.

"Claude, snap out of it! If Riordan really believes you killed Robert —"

"Moi?" he shrilled. "What about him? He's as much a suspect as I am now."

"What are you talking about?"

"Robert used to go to that club. Maybe he met Riordan there."

Robert had kinks — enjoyed his kinks — but BDSM? I couldn't see him putting up with the restraints and discipline of being a bottom — he wouldn't have been able to remember half the rules — and no sane person would allow Rob to be his Top.

"Come off it!"

"You come off it! Why are you defending the dude?"

"I'm not." Hastily I scribbled down the three Cat Who books and a copy of *The Murder of Roger Ackroyd*, took the customer's money, nodded thank you. She grabbed her books and stalked off.

"You are," Claude insisted. "You *are*. You've got a thing for that — that —" His French having failed him, Claude concluded, "fucking *oaf.*"

"Claude, just use your head for once."

"Sounds to me like *head* is what you're using."

"Give me a damn break!"

The dial tone met my ears. I ground the words I wanted to say between my teeth, then replaced the phone.

Glancing up, I stiffened. I hadn't heard anyone come in, but Bruce Green stood on the other side of the counter.

CHAPTER SEVEN

"**H**i," he said. "Can I buy you a cup of coffee?"

"Now is not a good time," I said.

If Green felt the frost in my voice he gave no sign.

"Trouble?" He nodded at the phone. "I couldn't help overhearing. The police again?"

"No. Look, I called *Boytimes*. They never heard of you."

Green regarded me, looking genuinely perplexed. If he was acting he deserved better roles than this. Then a slow tide of red swept across his rawboned features. "Uh, the truth is, I'm not on *staff* at *Boytimes*. I do freelance work for them."

"Yeah, right." I started to turn away and he grabbed my arm. Not roughly, but with force enough to stop me. I gazed at his hand. Fine dark hair sprinkled the back of his long strong fingers. His nails were trimmed, buffed, the cuff of his shirt snowy white. But what I thought was, *I bet you're hefty enough to stab a man to death and toss his body in a dumpster.* To say I was fixated was to understate the case.

"Did you talk to Kelly Abrahms, the managing editor? Or did you just talk to the switchboard?" His eyes were dark and sincere.

I shrugged. "I talked to a couple of people. I don't remember their names."

Green smiled. The smile was surprisingly attractive in his plain face. "Want me to show you my bylines?" His tone grew teasing. "Or better yet, my etchings?"

I found myself responding to the smile, although my suspicions were not completely allayed. I don't trust the media. Not even the gay media.

"No. But thanks."

"Listen, I'm serious," coaxed Green. "Give me a chance to explain over a cup of java." He checked his watch. "Or better yet, how about a real drink? I know this pub a few blocks from here. You'll like it. It's comfy. Cozy. We can talk."

Although he had removed his hand I still felt the warmth of his skin against mine. Maybe I did need to talk to someone — anyone — even a reporter. Or maybe I just found the guy attractive. It had been so long I hardly recognized the signals.

✻ ✻ ✻ ✻ ✻

The pub was called Doc and Doris's. It was decorated in a Scottish motif: red and black tartan carpet, blackened beams. And it was indeed comfy, cozy with giant leather booths for privacy and a roaring fire at the end of the room. I ordered a Drambuie, and Green ("Call me Bruce") had a Rob Roy. Bruce touched his glass to mine.

"From bad beginnings great friendships have sprung," he quoted.

"Cheers."

Bruce took a long swallow, set down his glass and leaned forward on his elbows. "I have a confession."

"Another one?"

He met my eyes. "I didn't lie to you, Adrien. I wanted to write your story for *Boytimes*. You may not like it, but I think I have a responsibility to our community. You're not the first gay man to be railroaded by the cops. Besides, think of the publicity for your bookstore."

"Is this supposed to be convincing me?"

He flicked me a look under his eyelashes. He had very long lashes. "Past tense. It turns out you're not the only gay man to attract the fascist eye of LAPD. Besides," he offered another of those engaging smiles, "in theory I respect the right to privacy for non-celebrities."

In theory but not in practice? I said, "There wasn't any story, Bruce."

"I wouldn't say that." He sipped his drink. "Don't misunderstand me; I did dig up everything I could about you. Everything the cops know, I know."

"What's to know? My life is an open book. No pun intended." I sat back, swirling the Drambuie, watching it catch the firelight. It had a soothing, near hypnotic effect. My nerves uncurled.

"Let's see. You're thirty-two years old. A Virgo. Unmarried. No children."

He paused. I had nothing to say.

"No priors. No convictions. Even your video rentals go back on time. Affluent, white and well-educated, you fit the old gay stereotype to a 'T'."

"That's the sweetest thing anyone's ever said to me."

Bruce chuckled. "See, that's a turn-on for someone like me."

What was someone like Bruce, I wondered?

I took in the expensive haircut, the just-right clothes, the manicured hands; I recognized the scent he wore. "The world's only patented fragrance," so the department store displays read. And if I wasn't mistaken he'd had his nose fixed a while back. He was a man who paid attention to details. A good trait in a journalist.

"Father deceased. Mummy is English. Formerly a dancer with the Royal Ballet. She never remarried. Question mark by Mummy. You graduated from Stanford University with a degree in literature, which is civilized but useless, but then you don't have to work for a living."

"You don't think so?"

Bruce studied me speculatively. "Orange groves and horse ranches on Daddy's side. Going by your TRW, no, I don't think so." He straightened his immaculate cuffs. "You currently live alone. Your former roommate, Mel Davis, has since moved to Berkeley where he teaches film studies."

Clark Kent had certainly done his homework on me — and I didn't care for it. "Am I right or am I right?"

I gave him a perfunctory smile. "I'm impressed."

He regarded me. "Actually, you're pissed. Why?" He seemed hurt. "I've told you I'm not doing the story. This is off the record. Just you and me."

I finished my drink. Bruce beckoned imperiously to the waitress. The minute she was out of earshot he said quietly, "I don't want to do or say any-thing to bitch this up."

I nearly said, "Bitch *what* up?" but he seemed genuine. I shrugged. "Okay."

After a moment his gaze fell. He said awkwardly, "Am I coming on too strong? I feel like there's kind of a connection between us. I felt it that first day. At the funeral. Is it just me?"

I opened my mouth, couldn't think of anything intelligent and, for once, closed it.

Bruce chinked the ice in his empty glass. "It's been a long time since I felt this way."

"I'm flattered." Mostly. Also vaguely alarmed. It had been a long time for me too. Mel hied off to his ivory tower five years ago. Hell, I hadn't had a date in eight months.

"But —?"

"No buts."

He laughed. After a second it clicked and I laughed too.

"Not on the first date anyway," agreed Bruce.

* * * * *

When I meet someone I always want to know who and what they read. A writer's natural curiosity. Bruce said he read strictly nonfiction. Mostly biography. Right now he was reading *Auden in Love,* which he offered to loan me when he finished.

Can this marriage be saved? I read mysteries. For one thing, it's my job. For another, it's what I like to read. One of my favorite crime writers is Leslie Ford. Ford was just one of the pen names of Zenith Jones Brown, an American who wrote prolifically from the '30s through the '50s. Her Grace Latham series is one of my never fail "comfort reads."

For some reason the fact that my favorite mystery writer should be a heterosexual woman irritated the shit out of Rob.

Not just a heterosexual woman, Adrien. A white, rich, Republican heterosexual woman.

Republican? Where do you get that?

You know what I mean.

No, I didn't a lot of the time.

Rob's own favorite mystery writer was Michael Nava. But any gay writer would do. Maybe he read my attitude as disloyal. Maybe having spent years of playing Happy Families, of pretending his square peg was comfortable in a round hole, Robert just didn't have any patience left. He was militantly gay: *We are at war, Adrien. We are under siege.*

I was thinking about it that night as I lay in bed skimming Ford's *Date with Death*. I looked across to the empty half of the bed and sighed. I laid the paperback aside — carefully, because the browned pages were fragile — and folded my arms behind my head, thinking again about Robert.

When I told Chan and Riordan and Claude and everybody else that Robert and I were never lovers it hadn't exactly been the truth. It hadn't exactly been a lie either. You couldn't call the panting, fumbling first sexual explorations of adolescence a love affair. But whatever you called it, Robert and I shared a lot of history, and the fact that we had matured into adults who couldn't understand each other didn't change that.

Robert believed no one could ever really know anyone else.

Come off it, Rob. Doesn't that depend on the person?

No. Because people don't see you. They see their perception of you. They see what they want to see.

Another cosmic rift between us. But maybe Robert did have more experience there than I. If Tara had really never suspected ...?

I considered what I knew of Tara. Not much. She had simply been an ever-present accessory of the teenage Rob. Like his Datsun B210. Or his fake ID. Always in the background, like in the yearbook photo. Thinking back, I was horrified at how careless — and callous — we'd been. And yet Tara said she'd never known, never suspected until they were married. Until, in fact, they were separating.

There's a reason whenever homicide occurs that spouses and ex-spouses are the hands-down favorite suspects of law enforcement. But there was no way Tara could overpower Rob, stab him to death and lift his body into a dumpster. Besides, she had been in Iowa.

Of course Tara could have an accomplice. I could picture the type: a manly, brawny regular guy who knew exactly how to take out the trash. That was the way he'd put it too, taking out the trash. Hell-hath-no-fury? Was that a realistic motive for murder? Divorce hetero style? But that would mean Tara was involved with another man even while she was begging Rob to come back to her.

Was she that devious?

Was she that sharp?

I snapped out the light, scooted down into the blankets.

Ex-lovers were another popular choice for homicidal maniacs both in fiction and real life. Robert had broken plenty of hearts, and in particular Claude's. But despite Claude's hard feelings, which he hadn't bothered to hide (and wouldn't he, if he had a murder to hide?), I didn't believe Claude had killed Robert. He was heavy and muscular enough, and the news about his violent youth nonplussed me, but I still couldn't credit the police's suspicion.

Because I didn't want to?

Or because my gut told me Claude's gay blade days were far behind him? Despite the bloodcurdling poetry, I didn't believe Claude could stab Robert to death. His pride had taken a beating, but did people kill over wounded pride? Claude was a gentle man. Sure he could get loud and emotional, but before Riordan had crossed our path I had never heard anyone accuse him of even so much as verbal cruelty. I thought of the many ways he cosseted me and other friends. I thought of his generosity: the ex-lovers he helped out, the free dinners he supplied to organizations like Project Angel Food, the donations he made to The Cause — whatever cause someone talked his soft heart into supporting.

I sure as hell couldn't imagine him premeditating a murder. Didn't the presence of the chess piece indicate premeditation?

All the same, where had Claude been that night? He must have had as lame an alibi as me, or the police wouldn't still be snooping around. Unlike me, Claude enjoyed a busy social schedule. He should have witnesses to his innocence standing in queue, but apparently not.

He was jealous. I did remember Robert commenting on that once. But then Robert thought anyone who couldn't cheerfully accept his revolving door relationships was insanely possessive.

Anyway, I couldn't think of any connection between Claude and chess. I doubted if he knew castling from cholesterol.

I snorted. Sat up and punched my pillow. I was still betting on the mystery man Robert had gone to meet that night. The man who had sent Robert roses. The man Robert had gone to meet when he walked out on me.

I tried to think back to the days before Robert had died. Had he said anything that might give me a clue? I considered snippets of overheard phone conversations. The sad truth was I'd been so busy bottling my anger at his haphazard work, his obvious indifference to the job, I hadn't paid much attention. I had noticed — and been irritated — by his sunny indifference in the face of my glowering disapproval. That in itself indicated his attention had been elsewhere, because when he had first returned to L.A. he had definitely been interested in picking up where we left off.

What if Rob's death hadn't had anything to do with romance, ill-fated or otherwise? If Rob had been in some kind of trouble, would he have confided in me?

I wasn't sure. He confided in me less and less. *You're turning into an old maid, Adrien*, he'd said when I lectured him about promiscuity in the age of AIDS.

Only ten percent of people infected with the virus even know they've got it, Rob.

It would have to be immaculate contagion in your case, wouldn't it, Adrien?

He hadn't told me he was having serious money trouble. That news had come from Claude, and he had assumed that I already knew.

But the eighty bucks missing from petty cash would not have solved Robert's credit problems. So what did he need the eighty for? My best guess: to take someone out. To buy someone dinner. It kept coming back to this unknown other. Mr. X.

Why hadn't Rob just asked for the money?

Because he didn't want to hear it, Adrien, I answered myself. Only he had to hear it anyway. And my last memory of Robert amounted to me calling him a liar and a thief, and Robert telling me to fuck off. Now there's a Kodak moment for you.

I sighed. Tossed against the pillows. I watched the shadow of lace curtains patterned against the wall. Listened to pinpricks of rain against the windows. The wettest winter since El Niño, everyone kept saying. That's something I missed, lying in bed listening to the rain with someone I loved. That's something I missed, having someone I loved.

But in the meantime there were still methods that worked. I rolled onto my side, face buried in the cool linen, one hand between my legs. Solo sex. The cheapest and safest of dates. I closed my eyes and Robert's face floated into my mind. I pushed it away. Thought of Riordan. Thought of a big hand wrapping around my shaft, sliding up and down, pumping hard … harder. The head of my cock leaked a single salty tear to slick my own hand's efforts. Yikes. Think of Bruce. Yeah. Better. Safer. Saner …

* * * * *

Tuesday afternoon Angus and I were sorting through a shipment from St. Martin's Press when he found the card slipped in between some copies of *Crime Scene*.

"This must be for you." He handed over a large, square envelope. I noticed the fingernails on both his little fingers were about two inches long. I tried to remember from my reading what that meant. Lead guitar or warlock? Or maybe just a nice normal cocaine addiction.

"Thanks." A plain white greeting-sized envelope. I opened it, drew out the large *In Sympathy* card. Red roses and a pair of praying hands. My own hands were none too steady as I opened the card. The inscription was standard fare. I'd sent something similar to Robert's father. Below in familiar black calligraphy someone had written:

Our acts our angels are —

For good or ill

"When did this come?"

Angus shrugged, having already lost interest.

"How long have those magazines been stacked there?"

"Since Saturday," he breathed.

I contemplated the black script. There was something about those lines. They were from a poem, I thought. Not Shakespeare; I knew my Shakespeare pretty well, thanks to old Jason Leland and *Murder Will Out*. Bacon? Marlowe?

I tried to remember what the note on the roses had read. Something about all things in their time.

I slid the card back into the envelope. Glancing up I caught Angus watching me with an enigmatic expression.

Angus could have slipped the card in there, I realized, and then pretended to find it. Tara had also been standing in front of the counter when I ran upstairs to get sodas for the kids. And Riordan had been in the shop on Saturday. Hell, Bruce could have slipped it in yesterday. For that matter dozens of people had stood by the counter, by the magazines. It needn't have been anyone I knew.

I had given Riordan the florist's card so that he could double-check whether there had been a screw up. Had he bothered to confirm one way or the other?

With a word to Angus, I went into my office and dialed the number on the card Chan had left me that first morning. I got the Hollywood Area Homicide Unit. Neither Chan nor Riordan was available. I left a message.

After I hung up I sat there idly tapping the card against the clock on my desk.

It occurred to me that I hadn't heard from Claude following our spat yesterday. That seemed odd.

It occurred to me that since the card had been left for me, there probably hadn't been any mix-up at the florists. The roses with their cryptic message had also been intended for me.

It occurred to me that Tara was right about possible mice. There was definitely a peculiar odor permeating the shop. Here in the office it was quite pungent.

It occurred to me that I didn't know what any of that meant, but I didn't like it.

CHAPTER EIGHT

In the week since Robert had died he had gone from second page news to a blurb filling space between the Robinson-May and Nordstrom shoe ads. The investigation was "ongoing" in the police vernacular.

On Tuesday night the Partners in Crime writing group met again. The main topic was still Rob's murder or, more accurately, the ensuing investigation. It seemed as though everyone had been visited by Chan and Riordan. I think for the most part they found it mildly titillating, and yet it did seem to me that I was being surreptitiously observed by my partners in crime. Was there something artificially eager in their conversation? Was there something awkward in the pauses?

Eight o'clock came and went with no sign of Claude. Grania's little cobblestones (she swore they were granola cookies) were handed out (although I didn't notice anyone risking their dental work on them), a gallon of coffee was poured, and the discussion moved from Robert to other topics.

"It's not a crime film, but the worst movie I ever saw," Max volunteered, "was *Bwana Devil* with Robert Stack."

"I saw that," Ted volunteered. "Sunday before last when I was waiting up for Jean."

"I was home last Sunday," Jean said instantly.

"Sunday evening before last, sugar pie." Yes, he calls her "sugar pie," and she calls him "honey bun." I don't get the pastry thing myself.

"I was home Sunday evening. It was Saturday evening I was out late," she protested. "I went to the movies with a girl from the office," she added for our benefit.

Oh yeah, the world famous I-was-at-the-cinema alibi. So had Jean been MIA on Sunday night or Saturday night? Not that it mattered to me, but it seemed to matter to Jean — and that in itself made it worth checking the previous week's TV Guide to see what night *Bwana Devil* had been televised.

That's how bad I had it. I was actually considering whether diminutive *Jean* could have slaughtered Robert. Never mind trivial considerations like motive. I mean, what possible motive could she have? I couldn't remember Robert ever having spoken to her.

"Yeah," Max was saying, apparently seeing nothing odd in Jean and Ted's tiny disagreement over her alibi. "The best part is toward the end when the lions have eaten this native kid, and the white hunter's wife screams at one of them, 'animal!' "

"You know, that movie is based on a true story," Jean informed Max.

Grania cut across his guffaws. "Are we going to wait all night for La Pierra?" Tonight she wore fatigue pants and a black chemise. Her wide mouth was outlined in poppy red. I wondered what the occasion was. Chapter meeting of her paramilitary cooking club?

Max stopped laughing and fixed her with his eyes.

"It's pretty damn rude. This is the Finches' night," Grania continued. "We all showed up for *Homicide les Hommes* or whatever it's called."

"Always thinking of others, eh, Toots?"

Grania flushed and tossed her head.

I wondered if this was the adult heterosexual version of pigtail pulling.

"We may as well get started," I agreed with one last look at the door.

Max smirked, swiped the last cookie and crammed it in his mouth. I wondered if that crunching sound we all heard was the last of his fillings.

"Well, we rewrote Chapter Two," Jean began, handing copies around the circle.

Someone groaned. I hoped it wasn't me. I wasn't sure.

Jean said defensively, "Well, we thought Claude made some good points about angle of entry and blood spatter patterns on a raincoat. And even a highly disciplined mime probably *would* scream —"

"So where *is* La Pierra?" Max interrupted, propping his feet on the long table.

Ted looked irritated. "Who cares? Jean is talking."

"Sorry, Jean."

Jean handed Max a copy. She and Ted performed a little You-First-No-You-First routine and Jean finally plumped down in the Sheraton chair.

"Jean will read tonight," Ted announced. He beamed at Jean.

Grania sighed in the manner of one exerting inhuman patience.

Jean read, and I sat there mechanically following along, all the while mentally turning over and over the Rubic cube of Claude's absence. Was he still pissed off? Despite leaving two messages, I hadn't heard from him since his phone call Sunday. That wasn't like Claude. His sulks never lasted more than a few hours.

Jean had a soothing voice. Perfect for reading kids to sleep.

Absently I made notes in the margin. Robert had been killed in the alley outside his apartment. Why? Why not in the apartment? Because he didn't bring his killer home with him? He had gone to meet someone. Yet he had come back to the Blue Parrot alone. Then, instead of looking for me, he had gone home. And someone had killed him out in the alley. What would lure Robert out into the alley?

Everyone turned to the next page. I followed suit.

Let's say I was a homicidal maniac who wanted to kill Robert someplace where we could have a little privacy. How would I do that? I might go up to his door very late at night and say, *Sorry about standing you up earlier but I had car trouble. In fact my piece of junk is parked out back blocking the alley right now.*

And Robert, not famous for caution or second thoughts, would be happy that I'd turned up after all, and naturally offer to lend a hand, and out we would go.

And when it was over, I could drive away in my bloodstained clothes unseen. Robert hadn't had time to put up much of a fight, but his attacker had not been willing to take any chances. Thumps and groans from the apartment next door might generate concern. Not so from an alley where bums and winos prowled.

I glanced up, caught Max staring at Grania intently. Feeling my gaze he gave me a cool look, turned to the manuscript he held. Grania pulled a pencil out of her hair, lined out what appeared to be a paragraph.

"Avery narrowed his eyes in thought at the inspector's question," read Jean. "Why would anyone want to kill a mime?"

"Go figure," muttered Grania.

Max smothered a laugh.

* * * * *

When the meeting was over and my partners in crime had left, I felt restless. I went around locking and bolting every conceivable entryway. Then I went upstairs and prowled around my flat. I turned on the computer, logged on and realized my brain had less going on than my screen saver. I signed off again, and popped *The Black Swan* into the video machine, went into the kitchen, and started stacking dishes in the dishwasher.

I needed to keep busy, needed to avoid thinking in order to relax enough to go to sleep without resorting to chemicals. I filled the solitude with the rumble of the dishwasher and Tyrone Power and Maureen O'Hara in a "Tale of the Spanish Main — when villainy wore a sash." I do like well-dressed villainy.

In the living room I stretched out on the floor and practiced deep breathing. I could feel the hard wood hitting all the sharps and angles of my bones. My spine felt kinked in a dozen places. Crikey. Middle-age was catching up to me. I stood with a groan and made myself go through the motions of my Tai Chi routine. Touch the South Wind. Touch the East Wind. The Tide Comes In and Out.

The funny thing was I did feel better after a few minutes. More tranquil. Like I could bend without breaking — emotionally and physically. I moved on to the hard style movements. Defy the Dragon. Defy the Leopard. Defy the Cops. I first started doing Tai Chi in college, and besides promoting a relaxed mental attitude — something I don't come by naturally — it does result in greater flexibility, coordination, and balance. Which is not to say it's everyone's cup of tea. I couldn't, for example, picture Detective Riordan giving up beating the shit out of a punching bag, or rowing frowning, sweat-streaked odometer miles in favor of Bird with the Folding Wing.

Thirty minutes and I headed for the shower. When I got out I noticed the light blinking on my answering machine. Abstracted as I'd been, it could have been flashing away all evening. I played back the message, but it was not Claude. Bruce Green had called. Despite his words he sounded unexpectedly diffident.

"Hi, Adrien. It's Bruce. I was just wondering when you'd like to have dinner? Give me a call."

I picked up the phone then slowly replaced it. Too late to call now. Besides...the habit of solitude had become ingrained. Other than the occasional twinge of loneliness, my single status was as comfortable as a mole snuggled in its hole — and as safe. Did I really want to risk that hard-won equilibrium?

I thought of the long, painful months after Mel left.

Wandering into the kitchen, I made a glass of Ovaltine, trailed back to the sofa and propped my feet on the sofa arm, watching the tail end of *The Black Swan*. Idly, I flipped through the yearbook Tara had left me.

Tara was right. Robert had belonged to just about everything going. There he was, left from bottom with the Tennis Team. I was scrunched in right next to him, smiling at some long forgotten joke. I recalled that photo had been taken a few weeks before I'd gotten sick.

Another photo of Rob with the Journalism Club — and I knew by that familiar grin he had just made some crack. Everyone around him was laughing. I turned the page and there was old Robert squiring Homecoming Queen Brittany Greenwahl. Man, they looked young. She smelled like cheese macaroni, he'd said. I'd been in the hospital for the junior prom, but that started me remembering. Hadn't there been some scandal right before summer vacation? Something to do with....

I flipped back to the index, ran my finger down the Clubs & Activities. Something for everyone: Choral, Creative Writing ... . Hey, how come I hadn't joined the Creative Writing club? Rob must have had another plan for us.

Wait, I had missed it. I started with the "C"s again. There it was: *Chess Club*. I found the page, and there in nostalgic black and white, just like a chess set themselves, were the five would-be Bobby Fischers: Robert Hersey, Andrew Chin, Grant Landis, Richard Corday, Felice Burns, and Not Pictured — Adrien English.

For the longest time I sat there staring at the photo, a funny flutter in the pulse point at the base of my throat.

The Chess Club? How could I have forgotten?

But how the hell could Robert's death have anything to do with what had happened back in high school?

Then again, both Robert and Rusty were dead. Murder and suicide. Two violent deaths. Surely that couldn't be a coincidence, not with Robert found holding a chess piece.

I tried to imagine one member of the Chess Club stalking the others. Talk about bad losers. Talk about delayed reaction. It was nearly fifteen years since we'd graduated. I rubbed my forehead as though that could stimulate my memory. It all seemed so long ago. I probably remembered the games more clearly than the players.

Yeah, now that I thought about it, there *had* been some kind of dust up. Something that happened while I'd been ill. Something that even Robert had been closemouthed about … .

I bolted upright at the clatter of trash cans in the alley below. Slapping shut the book, I walked back to the bedroom.

Pushing back the lace drapery, I stared down at the moonlit alley. Light lanced off the lids of the trash dumpsters against the back wall. Everything else was in shadow. I could just make out the edge of some trash cans stacked by the back entrance of the Thai restaurant next door. The trash cans were a point of contention. I didn't get why my neighbors had to have smelly trash cans by their back entrance (and mine) when the dumpsters were just a few feet away. The food scraps in the cans attracted cats and stray dogs and bums.

As I watched, starting to feel silly, there was another clang of metal on metal and then the reverberation of a lid hitting the pavement. Something round and shiny rolled into view and fell over, like a miniature moon.

A shadow detached itself from the others. I had to wipe the glass where my breath was fogging. The figure in the alley stepped back and looked up. It wore a mask. A grinning skull.

I gripped the window sill as my heart lurched and began that frantic ticking like a turn signal about to short out. I must be clearly outlined by the hall light behind me. I ducked back, like 14 point lace would be useful concealment. I risked another look.

Not sharing my fear, the figure in the skull mask waved to me. It was bizarre. A cheery little salute from the image of death. As I stood there gaping, the dark-clad apparition turned and sprang away down the alley with un-apparition-like vigor.

Belatedly my brain kicked in. I scrambled across the bed, found the phone and called the police. Then I lay flat on the mattress and gave myself a chance to catch my breath while I waited for the squad car to come.

Damn.

Just calm down.

Relax.

When I felt better, I pulled out a notepad from the side table and jotted the names of the remaining members of the Chess Club.

Andrew Chin

Grant Landis

Felice Burns

Me

I remembered Felice pretty clearly. She had been exceptionally poised and unreasonably focused for a girl her age. I seemed to recollect that she had been headed for med school. She could have married, but she might use her maiden name professionally. Perhaps I could track her through the AMA.

I barely remembered Andy Chin or Grant Landis. Chin, I thought, had been one of our stronger players, Landis one of our weaker. My own membership in the Chess Club had been brief and unremarkable. The life span of the Chess Club itself had been brief and unremarkable, now that I thought about it. Still there was no other connection I could think of linking me and Robert to "The Royal Game."

The fact that Rusty was also connected to the Chess Club seemed conclusive to me.

At last the squad car arrived. The uniformed officers took my report and poked around the alley and side streets, their flashlights picking out empty corners and cardboard boxes. A stray cat rocketed out of its hiding place like a cartoon character. Lights went on in the building across the cinderblock wall.

Though inclined to think "the disturbance" was kids playing a prank, the cops promised to swing around the block once on their way back to patrolling.

After they drove off, it seemed very quiet. Up and down the boulevard, the neighboring businesses stood dark and silent. Inside my building, aged joints popped and creaked, settling for the night — that would be the architectural joints, though mine weren't in much better shape.

I paced around, tried calling Claude. There was still no answer. I considered driving over there — I'd have liked the company — but I was too skittish to face the alley on my own.

Finally I fixed another cup of Ovaltine and curled on the sofa, rewinding *The Black Swan.*

* * * * *

By the next morning that indefinable bad smell in the shop had become a decidedly putrid stink.

"It smells like something died in here," Angus complained.

I don't know why it didn't click until then. I slammed down my coffee cup and hauled ass back to the office where I started shifting boxes, pulling stuff off the metal shelves.

"What's wrong?" Angus inquired from the doorway.

"Help me lift this."

Gingerly he picked his way through the rubble, helping me lower an old trunk with a broken lock to the floor.

The stench of decay was practically overpowering.

"Shit, man," Angus breathed. "There are ants everywhere." He wiped his hands on his 501s and stared at me. His eyes looked huge behind the specs.

I opened the trunk. There was a dead cat and many, many ants.

I closed the trunk.

Angus brushed by me. I could hear him vomiting in the bathroom off the office. After a moment I realized I was just standing there rubbing my hand across my mouth, listening to Angus. I phoned the police. By now I had the number memorized. The squad car showed up followed shortly by Chan and Riordan.

"Somebody doesn't like you, Mr. English," one of the uniforms remarked, closing his notepad on my second complaint in twenty-four hours.

They nodded in passing to Chan and Riordan.

"What's up?" Riordan asked.

"Someone put a dead cat in the trunk in my office."

Riordan and Chan exchanged The Look.

"Who?" Chan asked.

"Who? Is that a routine question? How do I know who? The same person who sent me black flowers and a sympathy card, and broke into my shop, and was skulking around the alley last night!"

"Am I missing something here?" Riordan asked his partner. Chan reached for a cigarette then recalled himself. He started patting his pockets for gum.

"If people would be candid to start with, it would help," Chan returned.

I gave an incredulous laugh. "*I'm* not being candid? I am a victim here. I am being stalked."

"Run that by me again," Riordan requested.

Actually until I put it into words the notion was nebulous, half-formed, but now I found myself stubbornly clinging to it. "I am being stalked."

"Who do you think is stalking you, Mr. English?" Chan asked politely, unwrapping a stick of gum.

"Whoever killed Robert." I caught sight of Angus loitering palely behind them. "Come upstairs. I have to show you something."

They followed me upstairs in silence. I could imagine the long-suffering looks exchanged behind my back.

In my living quarters I showed them Rob's yearbook. I told them what Tara had said about Robert asking her to mail it to him right before his death. I turned to the page with the Chess Club and pointed out Rusty. I explained about his taking a walk out a hotel window.

"I think his death might be related. Maybe he didn't kill himself."

"You're suggesting that someone killed Corday?" Chan was still neutral.

"I'm not sure what I'm suggesting. It's not impossible, is it?"

"Hard to say without seeing the police report," Riordan said.

Chan did a kind of double take in his partner's direction. "Mr. English," he said carefully, one eye on his partner, "What possible motive do you believe someone would have for killing members of your high school Chess Club?"

"I've no idea. I didn't participate in the Chess Club that long. But maybe one of the surviving members would know."

"*Surviving* members? Do you have some reason to believe something has happened to the other members?"

"Well, no, but isn't this too much of a coincidence?" I glanced at Riordan. He was looking around my living room curiously. I wasn't sure what he found so interesting — it would have been nice if he'd paid attention to what I was saying.

"No, not really, Mr. English," Chan answered. "In any high school graduation class there's going to be a number of deaths, suicides, even homicides by the time your tenth reunion rolls around. It's the law of averages."

"Whatever. What about this?" I thrust the "In Sympathy" card at Riordan, who seemed to recall himself.

He glanced at me under his brows, took the card, read it. He turned it over. Handed it to Chan. Said gravely, "It's not a Hallmark."

I grabbed the card from Chan, bending it in the process. "This is just one big fucking joke to you, isn't it? Well, it's my life being threatened. Robert is dead, remember, *detectives?*"

"Calm down, for Chrissake," Riordan muttered. He took the card back from me. "No one has threatened your life, have they?"

"It's implied by this card, by funeral flowers. Are you telling me it's not against the law to leave a dead animal on someone's property? That it's not illegal to break into someone's business? Obviously whoever burglarized my shop left this dead cat —"

"It's harassment, certainly," Chan agreed.

"*Harassment!*" I heard my voice shoot up like the Vienna Boys choir, and Riordan's eyebrows rose with it.

"Look, Mr. English," Chan began plaintively, "try to see it from our point."

"Oh, I get it." I stopped cold. "You still think I could be doing this to myself. That I'm trying to throw you off my trail. Red herrings, right?"

Chan interjected smoothly, "That's a good point, Mr. English. This book of yours that's going to be published; it's about a man who stabs to death an old friend, isn't it?"

I blinked once or twice. These two really did their homework. They must have learned about my book when they questioned the rest of the writing group — and really, the fact that they had questioned the writing group when Rob had spent so little time in it, had to be significant. They had to believe that either Claude or I was guilty.

"Actually, it's about a man who finds out who stabbed to death an old friend. He's an amateur sleuth."

"He's a homosexual." Thus spake Riordan. The kind of guy who probably slept in flannel sheets patterned with bears and pine trees and tiny lassos. A scratch-and-sniff-hygiene Real Man kind of guy. The kind of guy who circled the Chuck Norris marathon in the TV guide.

"You seem obsessed with my sexuality, Detective."

Something dark and shadowy slid across his eyes. I decided I didn't want to piss him off too much.

"Who identified Robert's body?" I asked suddenly.

"His wife."

"Tara? When?"

"She was here in L.A. when it happened," Riordan replied. "They were working on getting back together."

My jaw must have dropped. Chan stated the obvious. "You didn't know?"

"No."

Riordan, still holding the sympathy card, was running the edge underneath his thumbnail. He queried amiably, "Are you aware that Mrs. Hersey is the sole beneficiary of the million-dollar insurance policy left by Robert Hersey?"

"T-Tara?" I stammered. "Tara is Robert's beneficiary?"

Riordan looked at me and smiled oddly. "You didn't know."

"This is strictly confidential, Mr. English," Chan warned.

No it's not, I thought. This is another trap of some kind.

"Your life is not in danger, English," Riordan drawled.

I could feel myself turning red with anger.

"Did you actually bother to check out the florist?"

Riordan sighed. "Yes. The flowers came from the Conroy's on Balboa. It's a busy place. They were paid for in cash and no one remembers anything about the purchaser."

"So that's it? Did you bother showing pictures of anyone in case it jogged —"

"Pictures of *who*?" Riordan snapped. His anger was unexpected. "Yeah, as a matter of fact we showed *your* picture. Nobody remembered you."

Chan blew a gum bubble. Popped it. "Hersey's flowers came from the same place. One dozen red roses paid in cash. You got the deluxe arrangement, English."

"Lucky me. A stalker with good taste."

"Did Robert receive a card?" Riordan questioned.

"I don't know. He didn't say."

"What did he say? Did he seem nervous, preoccupied?"

"No."

"So he didn't feel threatened? Stalked?"

I stared at them.

"We'll be in touch," Riordan said.

CHAPTER NINE

I couldn't find anything to wear. Laundry had not been a major priority the last few days, and as I dug through the hamper seeking something I could iron into presentability I realized that Robert's death had put my own life on hold. It was like being shot but waiting to hear the crack of the rifle before you fell down.

I hadn't worked on my new book in over a week. In fact already the threads of plot seemed to be unraveling in my brain. I was afraid to look at the damn thing. And why had I ever thought of centering the plot around *Titus Andronicus?* I hate that play.

I had a stack of phone messages I hadn't answered, and so many DOROTHYL digests in my e-mail it was a wonder I hadn't crashed my computer. And, in case I wasn't feeling harassed enough, Jean and Ted were hounding me about putting out the bookstore newsletter the group had been discussing for the past six months. My feeble excuses were brushed aside and I was being dragged over to the Finches with the bribe of dinner.

"I know you, Adrien," Jean had said when she'd phoned a couple of hours earlier. "You're probably living on coffee and minute rice."

Hey, if God had intended me to cook he wouldn't have created Trader Joe's.

"Jean, you're confusing me with the helpless heterosexual male."

Jean just laughed. She's the most easygoing woman writer I've ever met.

Since my friends insisted on rallying round, the least I could do was wear a clean shirt.

In the end I had to settle for a white T-shirt under a black blazer and a pair of black jeans that I'd quit wearing because they made me feel I should be out waving down cars on Santa Monica Boulevard, except that they were too tight to walk in.

"Ooh, don't you look handsome," Jean chirped when Ted ushered me into their kitchen about forty-five minutes later.

Ted shoved a glass of red wine into my hand. "Good for the heart," he said, and gave my shoulder a nudge with his own.

I like Jean and Ted, don't get me wrong, but a little bit does go a long way. In their manuscript, *Murder He Mimed,* they have a gay character, Avery Oxford. Avery is thirty-two, single, with black hair and blue eyes and my wardrobe right down to my BVDs, which, in point of fact, Jean quizzed me about: "Do Gay Men Prefer Boxers or Briefs?" Every time I give an opinion I can see Jean perking up, taking mental notes. I'm terrified some day some fool may actually publish their magnum opus and Avery Oxford will be let loose as the quintessential gay stereotype.

"How are you holding up?" Jean asked, turning the heat off on the stove.

"I'm holding up." I sipped my wine, an unexpectedly smooth merlot.

Ted brought Jean a platter and she began spearing pork chops out of the pan. I was struck by their concord. I've never met any two people that seemed more truly two halves of one whole. The fact that they looked like fraternal twins heightened the effect.

"Gosh, it's sad," Jean said as Ted whisked the platter past me into the dining room alcove. "Robert was such a vibrant person. So … alive."

"Yes." I half-drained my wine glass. I really didn't want to think about Rob for one evening. "I'm sorry about the police. I hear they've been asking more questions."

Jean laughed. "Really, that's been kind of helpful. Getting to watch detectives on the job."

"What kinds of things did they ask you?"

Jean went over to the fridge. She sounded vague. "Oh, you know. The same kind of stuff they asked you, probably."

"They asked about Claude," Ted offered from the alcove. He was lighting candles on the dining room table.

"What's that? Oh." Jean took the salad out of the fridge. "Well, *Claude.* He is pretty emotional. Some of the things he says, you might think — I mean, *I* know he wouldn't hurt a fly, but if you don't know him you might think he's a violent person."

"Can I do anything to help?"

Jean smiled, shook her head, cocking her ear for Ted's next words. When none were forthcoming she called, "Are you thinking what I'm thinking?"

"Max?"

"Exactly."

I asked, "What about Max?"

Jean shooed me off into the dining room with one hand. With the other she balanced the salad bowl, waitress style. "Don't be shy, Adrien. Just sit anywhere."

I stepped into the alcove. One wall was solid books; the entire top shelf of the bookcase was lined with How to Writes. This was one of those small Westwood apartments made functional and attractive with the help of the local Ikea and gallons of peach and coral paint. Jean called it the "Southwest Look," and stuck cactus plants in every corner. I nearly backed into one as I made room for her to set the salad on the table.

"What do you think, Adrien?" Ted inquired as I sat.

I shook out an apricot colored napkin. "About what?"

"Max's homophobia. Do you think he could have killed Robert?"

It was clearly an academic question to them. I found that a bit scary. As scary as the notion that someone might want to kill me because of whom I'd slept with.

"Is Max a homophobe?"

"Of course," Jean stated unequivocally. She hopped up and disappeared into the tiny kitchen. "He hated Robert. *Hated* him."

"Well," Ted hedged. "Maybe homophobe is too strong. He doesn't hate *you.*"

"He just thinks you're seriously screwed up," Jean volunteered.

I wished I hadn't come to dinner.

"You're not eating," Ted said and passed the platter of chops my way.

Jean set a bowl of mashed potatoes before us and lit once more. She cocked her head like a friendly robin. "It does sound like a hate crime from what the papers say."

"All murder is a hate crime."

"No. Not really. Sometimes people are just in the way."

"Whoops! You're dry," Ted said and refilled my wine glass.

I drank up. Lowered my glass. "So what did the police ask you about me?"

Jean flew up again and dimmed the overhead light. In the moody candlelight they looked unnervingly like a pair of the Bobbsey Twins.

"Do you think he could have killed Robert?" they quoted together. Then they looked at each other and laughed merrily.

I opened my mouth, but Jean cut in, "We know you didn't."

"How do you know?"

"You just — you're not the type. You're too civilized."

"Doesn't that make me the prime suspect? By all the laws of mystery fiction? The least likely character?"

"That's fiction, Adrien," Jean explained kindly.

"Mostly English mysteries," Ted put in. "In those Golden Age classics it's always some smart-ass, over-refined *chap*. I guess half of them were probably supposed to be gay. Doesn't matter," he had to stop to chew and swallow. "Doesn't matter. Bad heart." He thumped his own chest for emphasis.

Not bad; just misguided, I wanted to say. I was still smarting over those smart-ass, over-refined, probably gay villains. As I trimmed the fat from my chop I became aware that Jean was watching attentively. She smiled, meeting my gaze. No doubt Avery Oxford would start exhibiting the "Continental" method of fork wielding. I couldn't wait for them to kill him off, but they couldn't ever seem to get beyond Chapter Three.

"If you don't mind my asking, what else did the police want to know?"

Jean and Ted exchanged a silent look.

She said off-handedly, "Oh, you know, they were asking about Claude and you. If you were an item. And if you needed money. And who you … well, you know, *dated*. We told them about the thing with Max."

For a minute I wondered if they thought *I'd* had a thing with Max. Exactly what were people telling the police?

"They didn't seem to find it very interesting," Ted opined. "Very close minded."

"We told them you couldn't have done it," Jean reassured me once more. "Claude is a different matter. He's homicidal if you argue cooking fats."

"I thought you didn't think Claude killed Robert?"

Jean looked up surprised. "Well, you never really *know* anyone, Adrien."

It was late when I left the Finches. I'd had several cups of coffee on top of half a bottle of wine; so I was driving more defensively than usual through Westwood. As ever the streets were crowded with college kids, the shop doors open and ablaze, theater lines wrapped around corners. On the radio Sarah McLachlan was singing "Building a Mystery," which seemed, in my alcohol-tempered state, significant.

I pulled up at a light, singing along under my breath. Two girls in fringed jackets walked arm in arm through the crosswalk. Sweet. Maybe the times were a-changin'. I drummed my fingers on the steering wheel, glanced at the jammed sidewalk outside a cinema.

Did a double take.

There in the queue for *Scary Movie* stood Detective Riordan, larger than life. Yes, it was definitely him. All six foot three of prime USDA beef in a leather bomber jacket. He had his arm around a red-haired girl and he was laughing down at her. Thanks to the music on the radio, it was like a scene out of a music video, with the shifting crowd cutting them off from view every couple of beats.

It struck me as more than coincidence. More like fate. Like when you've been thinking about someone so hard you seem to conjure him.

The light changed. The car behind me honked. I pulled away, my eyes glued to the rearview mirror till Riordan was lost to sight. No kidding; the guy had a life outside of being a cop. So much for Claude's leatherman scenario.

Right?

Unless the chick was a beard.

What the hell did I care? Unless there was some truth to Claude's theory about Riordan knowing Robert. About Riordan having some involvement in Robert's death.

Otherwise I had zero interest.

Riordan was not remotely my type. Even without the whips and canes and butt plugs. I don't understand the wish — let alone the need — to be dominated, controlled. Not presuming to judge, just not something I wanted for myself.

And yet.

And yet there was something about his strength, his arrogance, his sheer size that got under my skin. He probably couldn't even spell vanilla. He was probably selfish in the sack. Probably selfish and greedy and ... unsophisticated. And hung like a horse.

When I got home there was a message on my machine.

"Adrien? It's Bruce. I was hoping maybe I'd hear from you." Silence. Giving me a chance to pick up. "Call me sometime."

I hit rewind, listened to the message again. He had a nice voice. Maybe he sang in the shower. Would that be a plus or a minus? Was he a morning person or a night person? Did I have a preference?

I undressed, lay on the couch in my white boxer briefs balancing the phone on my stomach, and called Bruce.

"Well, hello there, stranger," he greeted me with pleasure. My heart warmed. Nice to be appreciated.

Bruce had just come in and wanted to talk. It went pretty well. No awkward pauses. We made plans for dinner the following night.

I spent Thursday morning letting my fingers do the walking through rows and rows of "Chins" in the White Pages. Two or three calls into it, my lame story about an alumni newsletter was coming more glibly, but I still wasn't having any luck locating Andy Chin. I didn't even know if he still lived in the state.

This, of course, is what comes of ignoring all those invitations to high school reunions.

"Darling, are the police after you?" my mother inquired when I picked up the phone that afternoon.

"No more so than usual. Why?"

"Because I had two police detectives to lunch yesterday —"

"*Lunch?* You fed them lunch?"

"Well, it was noon, darling. I couldn't very well eat in front of them."

"What did you serve them? Never mind. What did they ask about?"

"Grilled baby salmon, wild rice and asparagus with that luscious cream sauce that Maria makes," Lisa rattled off cheerfully. "They were quite civilized. For the most part. They asked about your friends. About Robert. When *did* Robert become gay, Adrien?'"

Through dry lips, I asked, "What else did they ask about?"

"Your inheritance."

"My what?"

"Your finances. That led to your inheritance. I told them about Mother Anna and that *insane* will. Splitting the money that way. I don't care what dear little Mr. Gracen says, the woman was *gaga*. Giving a boy your age that much money."

I waited for the pause and then got in, "Lisa, what did you tell them exactly?"

She said plaintively, "Darling, I've just *told* you. I explained you got half your money when you turned twenty-one, and shortly after *squandered* it on that grubby little shop."

I could feel sweat popping out over my forehead. "Lisa, I make a perfectly decent living."

My mother made a sound that from a lesser woman would have been a snort.

"What else did you tell them that was none of their damn business?"

"Don't start cursing, Adrien. They were rather nice. Very polite. Not at all what I expected."

I bet that worked both ways.

"And I did warn them darling that you were simply *not* up to being badgered. I told them what the specialist said — the first one, not that horrid quack from the Cleveland Clinic Heart Center. I think I made it very clear that if you were harassed any further I would set Mr. Gracen on them."

"Set Mr. Gracen ..." I hadn't the strength to finish it. Set loose the dogs of war in the form of "dear little Mr. Gracen" who was seventy if he was a day and could barely manage to dodder around the golf course? "Lisa, no one is badgering me. It's just routine."

"Say what you like, Adrien, but you looked very white and strained when you were here the other day. I really think you should consider coming home for a while."

Here we go again. "Lisa, I *am* home. Remember? I'm a big boy now. Don't start fussing."

"I never fuss." She grew lachrymose as another wrong occurred to her. "Did you know that Inspector Chan wants to write mysteries too? He was asking where you get all your ideas from. And you know, Adrien, I simply didn't *know*. I'm rather hurt that you've never let me read your book."

"It's not published yet." I was thinking rapidly. "Lisa —"

"Anyway, don't worry," she reassured. "I pointed out that you could have no *possible* motive for killing poor Robert Hersey."

"Did you mention to them when I get the balance of my money?"

"When you turn forty? It's none of their affair."

I sighed. "Well, at least they provide medical coverage in prison."

"That's not funny," Lisa said sharply. "It's in extremely bad taste."

"I know. Sorry."

She hung up, which is her jolly way of having the last word.

* * * * *

The conversation with Lisa convinced me that if I didn't come up with a suitable alternate, I was destined for San Quentin and an orange jumpsuit. Orange is not my color, and I've never wanted to go steady with a guy with hair on his back.

It wouldn't take the dynamic duo of Chan and Riordan long to establish that I was over-extended financially. Nothing too serious when you consider the average American is four paychecks from the street, but inheriting a "sizable" life insurance policy would have eased things up considerably. I knew that Chan and Riordan speculated that I had believed myself Robert's beneficiary. That gave me a motive. A strong motive.

In Leslie Ford mysteries money is nearly always the motive. But it's not the only motive. Not in real life. I could think of other motives. Maybe they didn't make sense to me, but the news is full of people killing each other for reasons that seem senseless. Senseless violence? I suppose it must make sense to the perpetrator.

It was in this mood that I went to see Max.

Max lived in a small house on the wrong side of Ventura Boulevard. Seashell wind chimes hung on the front porch and a white-muzzled German Shepherd barked at me through a wooden gate.

I walked up the steps, rang the bell, and Grania Joyce opened the door.

I think we must have looked mutually startled. She recovered first, holding the screen open for me and inviting me in.

"Max!" she yelled toward the back of the house.

"Sorry for barging in."

"You're not." She was wearing an oversize sweatshirt which read, *Pasadena City College*, and a pair of granny glasses. If she had shorts or anything on underneath Max's old sweatshirt, I couldn't see them. "We were brainstorming," she said. Then she winked at me and strolled off to vanish into the bathroom.

The front room had been done in a minimalist bachelor-pad motif. There were a couple of antique typewriters on some oak bookshelves, a couple of wide comfortable chairs and sofas, a vintage Varga poster over a fake fireplace.

A moment later Max appeared, tucking a flannel shirt into his faded jeans.

"Yo, Adrien. What's up?"

"Two things," I said. "First off, you and Grania and the Finches are set on this newsletter. I'll finance it, but that's the extent of my involvement. I don't have time for another project. The Finches want to contribute with reviews, but they don't want to manage the thing. Either you or Grania will have to play editor."

Max scratched his chest reflectively. "Grania, huh?"

"You can always arm wrestle her for it."

Max laughed as though I'd said something witty. "About Grania," he said. "We're collaborating. I'm helping her with her male point of view."

I couldn't help it. "Oh yeah? What's she helping you with?"

"Sentence structure." His grin was wry. He shifted his weight. "Sure. What the hey, I'll edit your newsletter. Why not?"

"There's something else." Mentally I closed my eyes, pinched my nose and jumped. "A day or two before he died, Rob was talking to me about something that happened between you two, something he regretted."

Max hadn't moved. His narrowed eyes watched me closely.

"Yeah?"

"I thought you should know that."

For a moment Max didn't move. Then he snorted. "Bullshit. I don't know what he told you, bud, but that asshole didn't have any regrets. He was *sick*."

"Because he was gay?"

"No, because he was sick. Okay? I'm sure he didn't give you the whole picture. I mean fags, I just don't get it. What is wrong with you guys?"

"Nothing that I'm aware of."

"Yeah, well there's a difference of opinion there, no offense. And Hersey — that little shit follows me into a pub one night and wants to get it on in the john. He won't take no for an answer." Max laughed angrily. "I mean it was fucking ridiculous! The pip-squeak. And the rougher I get the more he likes it! Did he mention that?"

"No."

He shook his shaggy curls. "It makes me want to puke to think about it. The shit he was saying. His face —" Max shuddered with revulsion. "Did he tell you I shoved his head down a toilet?"

I felt numb in the face of his naked loathing. It was like picking up a rock and glimpsing the slimy things that lived beneath. After a moment I said, "No."

"I did. Since he liked to stick his face in assholes it seemed appropriate." Whatever he read in my face caused him to add harshly, "I have no regrets. He was out of control."

"Didn't it occur to you that maybe he needed help?" Despite myself I was angry.

"He was beyond help."

"He is now, isn't he?" I pointed out bitterly.

CHAPTER TEN

The phone rang, splitting the quiet of the back office.

For a minute I thought the whispering on the other end of the line was my stalker.

"Hello?" I asked sharply, "Who is this?"

"I've got to talk to you."

"Claude? Where the hell have you been?"

"Jail, if you must know."

"J-Jail?" I think I stammered it. "Why didn't you call me? Why didn't you let me know?"

"I wasn't under arrest. They were holding me for questioning."

"Technically that *is* an arrest."

"What*ever!* I wasn't formally charged. Shit, Adrien, will you focus here?" No trace of the gay Parisian now. He sounded angry and accusing. "I'm not going to jail, man. Not for anyone."

"Why would they arrest you?"

"Because they think I did it! They brought every knife in the café in for tests. Listen to me. I need money."

"How much money?"

"Serious money. As much as you can lay your hands on."

"Have you spoken to a lawyer yet?"

"I don't need money for a lawyer, man, I'm splitting."

"Wait a sec. What do you mean you're splitting? Where are you?"

"That doesn't matter. I'll be at the café at 6:00."

Bruce. I was supposed to meet him at 6:00. Shit. I thought fast.

"Claude, that's less than an hour. It's going to take some time to get the money together. Why don't we meet somewhere and talk?"

"I don't have time, Adrien. I know a man with a private plane who can sneak me out of Burbank Airport, but it's got to be tonight."

My inner child was hugging himself and keening, "This can't be happening!" With comparative calm, I said, "Claude, you don't know what you're doing."

"Are you going to help me or not?"

He sounded like a stranger. Almost threatening. "Of course I'll help you, but —"

"Good. Bring the money to the restaurant at six. Come alone."

I tried to joke. "This sounds like one of those scenes in a slasher movie —"

Dial tone.

* * * * *

I called Bruce and got his machine. I disconnected without leaving a message.

By the time I finished pulling on a pair of khakis and a V-neck sweater over my white T-shirt, it was five-thirty. I tried Bruce again. After a succession of clicks and static, while I mentally bit my nails, Bruce picked up.

I said awkwardly, "Bad news. I've got to take a rain check on tonight."

Silence.

I could hear the line crackling.

"Are you there, Bruce?"

"Yes," he said ungraciously. "Why?"

"Why?"

"Why are you canceling?"

"I can't — this sounds ridiculous, I know. I can't explain why. Yet."

Another silence. A very bad connection. In more ways than one.

"Yeah. Okay. Well, another time." He sounded extremely cool.

"Bruce, it's something I can't get out of."

"Sure. No problem."

It obviously was a problem. I said, "I'm free Friday. Tomorrow night."

"I'm not."

Ouch.

"I'll call you," I said to the unfriendly static.

"Do that."

Click.

I broke every speed law and ran three ambers in my haste to get across town before Claude did something really dumb.

When I got to the restaurant, which should have been packed at this time of the evening, a placard in the window read CLOSED. I looked up. Tire treads of black clouds tracked ominously across the gray sky. More bad weather on the way.

I parked in the back and walked around to the rear entrance. I tried the door. It opened with a screech of hinges more suitable for a haunted house than haute cuisine. Memories of all these scenes from all those movies where the dumb heroine goes to meet the murderer in an abandoned warehouse or a park at night or the backstage of a theater flickered through my brain. Except this was Claude I was going to meet, and I knew he hadn't killed Rob.

"Claude?" I stepped into the kitchen, my eyes adjusting to the gloom. Rows of kettles and pots gleamed dully above the counters. The smell of disinfectant hung heavily in the air mixed with the ghostly memory of garlic, basil, thyme — and a hint of cigarette smoke.

I wandered through the counters and cutting boards, guided by the emergency lights to the dining room. A tiny red dot in the darkness pinpointed Claude's whereabouts.

"What are you doing sitting here in the dark?"

He must have been lost in thought because at the sound of my voice he started and called out shakily, "Adrien? Shit, man. You scared me."

I started across the black ice floor. "Who'd you think it was?"

"That cop. Riordan."

I sat down across from Claude in the booth. He was like a phantom in the gloom, just a glimmer of eyes and teeth and the glint of the glass at his elbow.

"Did you bring the money?"

"No."

"Jesus fucking Christ! Why not?"

"Because I don't have it," I explained patiently. "If I did have it I wouldn't have brought it."

"*Why?*" Claude cried. "Why?"

"Because I'm trying to keep you from self-destructing. Because I'm your friend."

"*Friend?* You just signed my fucking death warrant. That cop is going to kill me. He killed Robert and he's going to kill me."

I ran both hands through my hair. "Would you listen to yourself? Why would you say that?"

"Because he *told* me." He stubbed the cigarette out in the ashtray.

"He told you he killed Robert?"

"He told me he was going to kill me."

"When?"

"Right before the pigs turned me loose."

"Those were his exact words? I'm going to kill you?"

"Yes! Yes!" Claude's shadow moved and I saw the glitter of wet on his cheeks. "Adrien, I'll give you the title to this place. You know what it's worth. I can't go back to prison. *Please.*"

I covered his hand with mine. "Is it prison or Riordan you're afraid of?"

"Both."

"Listen to me. If you run, it's as good as a confession."

"I didn't *do* it!"

"I know. But it won't matter. You'll look guilty all the same. They'll arrest you and you will go to jail. I think they can extradite you from France."

"They would have to find me first." He wiped his cheeks with the back and then the palm of his hand. Picked up his glass.

"I can't believe we're even discussing this. Don't you understand? They had to let you go because they don't have enough to hold you."

"But they'll find it."

"They can't find what doesn't exist." I hesitated. "Right?"

Claude drank from his glass, set it down hard. Nodded. "Right. Okay." He nodded again, sucked in his breath. "But I am *begging* you, Adrien ... ."

"I don't have it."

He stared. "You could get it. Your mother —"

"I'm not asking my mother."

"A couple of thousand. That's all I'm asking. I know you have that much."

"Didn't you hear what I said? If you run, it's all over."

"What did you come here for?" Claude demanded loudly. He shoved the table at me, catching me hard below the ribs.

"Damn it!" I shoved the table back and slid out of the booth. "I'm trying to keep you from wrecking your entire life. I'm trying to keep you from losing everything you've worked for."

"Yeah, well with friends like you, who needs enemies?" Claude surged to his feet. Jabbed his hand toward the kitchen. "Go! Get the hell out! I don't need you. I don't need your kind of help."

"Sure," I shot back. "You've got it under control. I can see that." I gestured to the sign in the shuttered windows and him skulking in the dark.

"Fuck off!" he shouted. He picked up the ashtray and threw it at my head. I mean, pitched it with a force that would have knocked me cold if it had connected. But I ducked, and the ashtray hit the post so hard it shattered.

I gave Claude the universal sign for *au revoir asshole* and headed for the door.

"You little prick, Adrien," he called after me. "I'd have done it for you."

I kept hearing his words over and over as I drove away. *I'd have done it for you.* And I knew it was true. Were our positions reversed, Claude would have done whatever I asked. Who the hell was I to decide what was best for him?

Halfway home I swung the Bronco around and started back for Café Noir.

It took a while to find an ATM. I pulled two hundred from the business account, another two hundred from my personal, and finally the last eighty bucks I had in my savings. It wouldn't take him far but it was the best I could do.

By then it was dark in the empty parking lot. The sagging power lines hummed overhead as I got out of my car.

I slipped through the back entrance, found myself in what Wilkie Collins would have called "complete obfuscation." I felt around the wall, found the light switch. The fluorescent lights threw hard white light on steel sinks, polished floors, spotless trash pails.

It was absolutely still.

For a moment I thought Claude must have left — but he would never forget to lock the café. Not even if he was never coming back.

I opened my mouth to call out. Some instinct held me silent. From the dining room I heard a faint sound. Slowly I walked to the doorway and, as I reached it, someone hurtled through, crashing into me, knocking me to the glossy floor.

I looked up, bewildered. I had a glimpse of dark raincoat, a hat pulled low, a skeleton face, a butcher's knife. A vision straight out of a Wes Craven movie.

Terror galvanized me. I rolled over, scrambled under the nearest table, grabbed for a chair to use as a shield. But the dark figure was running for the back door, raincoat flapping like a scarecrow's overcoat.

Though my heart was in full gallop, my mind was strangely cool. Each moment, each detail, seemed clear and focused as I crawled out from under my flimsy fortress of table legs. I considered and instantly discarded giving chase.

"Claude?"

No answer but a strange sighing like the tide soughing against the shore. I felt my way through the gloom to the wall switch. Mini white bulbs like Christmas tree lights flared on all over the room like tiny stars.

Claude lay by the front door, a dull puddle widening beneath him, slowly covering the black and white checked floor. I found my way to him. His pastel silk shirt was splotched with red; violent polka dots.

At that point my brain shut down. I was seeing it, I was taking it all in, I kept twisting the key but the engine wouldn't turn over. I dropped down on my knees. I touched Claude's face and I noticed detachedly that my knuckles were grazed.

Claude's eyes, which were staring at nothing, blinked.

He opened his mouth and blood spilled out in a gush. I put my hand over his mouth as though I could stop it from pouring out. I heard myself whispering, "Oh God, oh God, oh God...."

* * * * *

Police car lights cut swaths of red and blue through the thick night. There were uniforms everywhere, making room for each other as they passed in and out the narrow rear entrance of Café Noir. I leaned against a police car. From inside, the radio was transmitting to nobody. I hugged my arms against the cold and my nerves.

Riordan strode out of the kitchen doorway and spotted me. His shoes crunched on gravel as he approached.

I remembered that Claude said Riordan threatened to kill him. I hadn't believed him. Now Claude was dead.

"How are you doing?"

I nodded tightly, having found that little movements made it easier to hide the fact I was still shaking.

He scrutinized my face. "How's the heart?"

"Takes a licking, keeps on ticking."

He continued to stare. Asked curtly, "You want my jacket?"

I didn't think I heard him right so I gave my stock response. "Thanks. I'm fine."

"Do tell." He shrugged out of his suede jacket, tossed it to me. It felt like something newly dead hanging there in my hands. After a moment I fumbled my way into it. It was warm from his body and carried the scent of his soap.

"When did you hurt your hand?"

I looked dully at my scraped knuckles. "I don't remember. When I crawled under the table, I guess."

"Uh huh." He started to say something, then seemed to change his mind. "Feel up to telling me what you saw?" His breath hung in the light from the parking lot overheads.

I nodded toward one of the uniforms. "He took my statement."

"Now tell me."

I told him what I'd seen. He took it in, not taking notes, just nodding slowly.

"Skull mask? You mean like the mask you saw on the prowler outside your apartment?"

I assented.

"Or do you think you saw something, say a white ski mask, and your mind made the connection?"

"No."

"You said yourself it all happened pretty fast."

"I know what I saw. A skull mask. Like you buy at Halloween. The same mask. The same man. Hefty. Your height. Your build." I was having trouble controlling my voice.

Riordan's eyes flickered. "Okay. Bring it down a notch, Adrien."

"See, I have this problem," I told him. I told myself to stay cool but my hands balled into fists and my voice rose. "There is such an obvious link between everything that has happened that a blind man could see it, but somehow *you* don't see it. So I am asking myself, *why* don't you see it? Because you don't want to? Or because you don't want anyone else to?"

"Lower your voice."

A plain blue sedan pulled into the parking lot, shelling gravel, rolling up beside us. Chan got out in a cloud of tobacco smoke, ground a cigarette underfoot. He looked even more tired and depressed than usual.

Riordan walked over to him. They conferenced briefly. Riordan hiked a thumb over his shoulder at me. Chan nodded politely. I nodded back. Crime scene etiquette, I guess.

Chan and Riordan disappeared into the kitchen. A few minutes later a gurney bearing a black body bag was wheeled through the doorway.

I closed my eyes. Immediately I saw Claude's mouth open and blood spilling out. I scrubbed my face with both hands.

More time passed.

The adrenaline which had originally kept me going seeped away, leaving me cold and sick and exhausted. I'd have given anything just to sit. I considered dropping down on the parking lot gravel and leaning back against the police car tire. From the kitchen I listened to raised voices. One of them was Riordan.

Finally a young woman in uniform with French-braided hair came out. "Mr. English? I'm Officer Montoya. Detective Riordan has instructed me to drive you home now."

"Thanks. I can drive myself."

She was polite but firm. "You may not realize it but you're still in shock, sir. Best to let someone else drive you."

I decided this was probably their means of making sure I didn't make my break for the border.

"What about my car?"

"The Ford Bronco? My partner, Officer Lincoln, will drive it back for you."

Thus the prim and lovely Officer Montoya escorted me back to Pasadena and saw me to my door like the little gentleman she was.

"Would you like me to check the premises, sir?" One small hand rested on her night stick.

I shook my head. "Thanks anyway."

"Sure?" She smiled. It reminded me of the professional smile nurses give you when they see you're starting to fray around the edges.

"Yeah. I'm sure."

"Lock yourself in, sir."

"You betcha."

Officer Montoya strolled confidently off into the night and I locked the door against the darkness, against the unknown. Locked myself in with the silence and memory.

CHAPTER ELEVEN

The answering machine was winking at me as I shrugged out of Riordan's jacket and hung it on the iron coat stand.

I hit Play. A pause and then Bruce's voice said awkwardly, "I guess I was kind of an asshole earlier. If you want to call me I'll be home all night."

I called him. He picked it up on the fourth ring just as I was getting ready to hang up.

"Hi. It's me."

"Adrien." He cleared his throat nervously. "I hoped you'd call."

"I'm sorry about tonight. It was unavoida —" My voice gave out right then and there.

Bruce made alarmed noises. "What is it? The cops? What's wrong?"

It took a minute or two but finally I managed to be coherent.

"Adrien, my God," Bruce kept murmuring while I told him in terse sentences what had happened. "My God, Adrien. You could have been killed."

I closed my eyes, resting my forehead on my hand.

"Are you sure you're all right?"

"Yes."

"You don't sound all right. Do you want me to come over?"

"No. No, I shouldn't drag you into this."

"Yes, you should."

I was torn between guilt and relief. I thought I'd go nuts if I had to spend the night alone.

"Give me thirty minutes."

"You don't have to."

"I want to."

* * * * *

His body was beautiful: long-limbed, strong and beautiful. It felt good rubbing naked against mine. Everything he did felt good, despite the fact that it had clearly been a long time for him as well.

Our cocks slid together, the pleasurable scrape and thrust. Like bucks locking velvet-covered antlers in the spring. Testing, pushing.

Bruce's hand closed around my dick, working us together. Rigid thickness poking belly and thigh, rolling against each other.

"Do you like this?"

"God, yes."

"Good. I aim to please." He did too, despite the fumbling, the lack of choreography, the absence of what Mel used to call "simpatico." We were groping our way through the dark, literally, trying to find each other.

His mouth found mine, hot and wet. Hungry. I liked the hunger. Feeding it left me no time to think. I opened up, let his tongue shove in, let him explore. His fingers dug into my shoulders wanting closer, needing closer. I pressed closer, arched against him. He humped furiously. I rocked my hips welcoming the release roiling up inside. It was okay to take this. He needed it just as much as I did. His desperate cries spilled into my mouth. I kissed him, hips jerking. We pounded against each other and then he was coming, wet heat filling his condom. He groaned, his hand clenching spasmodically around my shaft. I groaned too, twisted, ground my hips. My balls tightened, my whole body stretching bow tight — and then that singing release.

"Tell me what you're thinking," he asked later.

"I'm not thinking. It's wonderful." *You think too much,* Robert had said. *You analyze everything to death,* Mel had said. I closed my ears to Mel's voice, to the memory of Robert. I gave myself to the moment, rubbed my cheek against Bruce's chest feeling the soft wire of his black hair. His arm tightened around my shoulders. I nestled into him, kissed his nipple.

"Can you see in the dark?"

"Hmmm?"

"I used to have a Siamese cat with eyes just the color of yours. He was the prettiest thing." He had that chatty note in his voice, the rare guy who is energized by sex. Not me. A police raid wouldn't have kept me awake at that point. Feeling safe and comfortable and warm, I let go.

Warm blood soaking the knees of my khakis, blood sticky on my fingers. Claude's eyes focused on mine, beseeching, trying to tell me...what?

"Who?" I whispered.

Claude's face shuddered. His whole body shuddered, the red slices welling blood, little mouths trying to speak. His lips unstuck. A gush of blood, bright red blood splashing out. A gurgling wet sound as he struggled...

"Jesus!" I sat bolt upright, lungs laboring, heart racing in blind terror.

There was commotion beside me. Books sliding off the bedstand as Bruce flailed around trying to find the lamp.

The light came on, rocked wildly, throwing menacing shadows before Bruce steadied it.

"What's wrong?" His lank hair was flattened to his head. He fingered it out of his eyes, staring at me. "What's the matter?"

It took a second to get my breath. I waited to see how upset about all this my heart was going to be. Finally I exhaled and leaned back cautiously into the pillows.

I shook my head. "Nightmare. Sorry. I'm okay now."

He was frowning. "What did you dream?"

"I don't remember." I nodded to the night table. "Could I have some water?"

Bruce picked up the glass of water, handed it over. I met his eyes and looked away. He looked out of place in my bed with his heavy three o'clock shadow, the brown protuberant nipples against his white skin. He looked... strange. It came hard to me that this was because he was ... a stranger.

"Talk to me," urged Bruce. "What the hell did you see tonight?"

"I just want to sleep. Okay?"

He nodded slowly. Took the glass from me. Pulled me into his arms cautiously as though he sensed I might resist.

He fell asleep long before I did.

I was letting Bruce out the front entrance when Riordan showed up early the next morning.

Natural enemies, the Press and the Police — they gave each other wide berth like well-trained but suspicious dogs.

I could see Bruce was hoping for a farewell smooch. I felt uncomfortable under Riordan's sardonic eye — what the hell was he doing there so early, anyway? I returned Bruce's embrace as stiffly as a Ken doll without the bendable knees.

"I'll call you," Bruce said, releasing me.

I nodded.

"Well, well," Riordan commented, clomping up the stairs behind me.

I ignored him, went into the kitchen and poured myself a cup of coffee.

"Sugar. No milk," he requested, pulling a chair from the table.

I poured him coffee. He took the cup in two big hands manly-man style. He looked like I felt, as though he hadn't slept all night, but he'd at least had time to shave and comb his hair.

He wore jeans, a gray sweatshirt and Reeboks, as though he had been on his way to the gym. Now that was kind of curious. He wasn't dressed for work and he had been lurking outside my shop at the crack of dawn. Early for a social call. Was he planning to knock off a potential witness?

"For the record," he began crisply, "There was no chess piece at the scene. We vacuumed it. Twice."

"Maybe I interrupted him before he could plant it."

"Maybe. But you didn't go to high school with La Pierra did you? La Pierra was never a member of any Chess Club?"

"No."

He sipped his coffee. Felt his point had been made, I guess.

Two separate killers preying on the gay community at the same time? I didn't buy it.

I said, "Maybe Claude was killed for another reason."

"Like?"

"He thought he knew who killed Robert."

"And that would be —?"

"You."

He was expecting this it seemed. His lips quirked in a half smile. "You do have balls, English." He took another swallow of coffee.

When nothing else seemed forthcoming I said, "Claude said you were gay."

This did get a reaction, although not what I expected.

"Gay." Riordan made a sound of disgust. "What a stupid term."

"What do you prefer?"

"Homosexual. Having sexual desire for those of the same sex."

"Yeah, such a mouthful though."

He slanted me a tawny look. "You don't seem surprised."

"I've had time to adjust to the idea."

"Me too, but it still comes as a shock."

When he moved, the outline of the powerful muscles in his arms and shoulders was plainly visible beneath the soft material of the sweatshirt. Same with the taut outline of his thigh muscles in those comfortably faded jeans. He would have made quick work of Rob or even Claude. He'd make quick work of me, no doubt, but somehow the fact that he smelled like deodorant soap and April-fresh fabric softener disarmed me. He smelled — and looked — like he grabbed his clothes straight out of the hot dryer. The sad thing was the overall impression was as groomed and confident as Bruce who spent three times the effort and money in getting that I-was-an-International-Male-model effect.

Life ain't fair.

I asked, genuinely curious, "How do you function? Does anyone know?"

"No. I kill everyone I fuck," he said derisively. "What do you think?"

"I mean anyone close to you. Family or friends?"

He met my gaze levelly. "No. And no one's going to." That was certainly straight enough for anyone.

"Is that a threat?"

"Do you really think I killed La Pierra?" He seemed amused.

"He said you threatened him."

"Oh, I did. And I meant it. It's as much as my life is worth out there." He jerked his head indicating the mean streets of Old Pasadena I suppose.

"What do you do? You date women?"

"I like women." After a moment he added wryly, "I just like men better."

I stared, trying to make sense of him. Now I knew why that old Sarah McLachlan song had seemed so appropriate. Especially the line, "You're so beautiful. A beautiful fucked up man." That about summed it up.

"So, do you have relationships with men?"

"Relationships?" He was sneering openly now. "Yeah. I have relationships with men. My father, my brothers, my partner. I have sex with queers. Don't confuse the two."

"Queers and men?"

"Sex and relationships."

"You've never had a healthy, satisfying homosexual relationship." It wasn't a question, but he answered anyway.

"That's a contradiction in terms."

Probably for him it was. If Claude was right, Riordan's playground was the dark world of S/M. Masters and slaves. Pain and bondage and humiliation and punishment — everything he felt he deserved, no doubt.

"Claude said you're into the whole leather scene. That he used to see you at a club called Ball and Chain."

His eyes were very green as they held my own. If this was the secret he had killed to protect, I had just put the finishing touches on my death warrant.

"Is it true?"

"Why? Looking for a sponsor?"

"I'm strictly a safe sex kind of guy."

"Yeah?"

I didn't understand that odd smile. Maybe he thought finding a guy leaving my apartment in the a.m. was a normal occurrence for me.

I was afraid to ask. I asked anyway. "What about Robert?"

"What about him?"

"Did you know him?" What I meant was, *did you kill him?*

"No."

I don't know if I believed him or not. I wasn't sure why he had revealed as much as he had to me. International Coffee Moment? Or because there was simply no one else in his life he could confide in? I couldn't imagine what it would be like trying to live under so much pressure, the strain of a double life. Small wonder if he wasn't schizoid.

He said casually, "By the way, we ran that card for fingerprints. Clean — other than yours."

"Mine?" Where would he get a comparison set of my fingerprints? I opened my mouth to ask, then caught his expression.

"Rob's apartment," I said. I remembered that before we left he had picked up my glass and carried it to the kitchen. At least that's what I'd thought; apparently the glass and my gloves had been removed for evidence.

As though I hadn't spoken, he added, "The flowers were a dead end."

"I hate for you to keep wasting your time. Maybe you should just plant evidence against me."

He let that go too. "It's interesting about the cat, though. It had been asphyxiated. It was too old and well-fed to be a stray. Any of your neighbors missing a cat?"

"I don't know." I dragged my thoughts back from the realization that the bastard had taken advantage of my moment of weakness. Why not? He was a cop and I was his numero uno suspect. This was a good reminder that I could not let my guard down with him. "Asphyxiated, huh?"

"Right." He watched me speculatively.

I said, "There's a Thai restaurant next door. If someone's missing a cat, you should probably talk to them."

His laugh sounded like it caught him off guard.

"I didn't kill someone's cat and stow it in the stockroom to lend weight to my story of being stalked."

"It does seem unlikely," he admitted.

I said, "Thanks for that much. So why didn't this freak chop the cat up too?"

"Maybe he liked the cat," Riordan commented. "Maybe he's kind to small animals and little old ladies."

"Then he wouldn't be the normal serial killer."

"Normal serial killer …" he repeated thoughtfully.

Was I totally off the mark? Shortly before his death Robert had been romantically involved with someone none of his friends knew — someone who might or might not be his killer. The same person who had killed Robert had broken into my shop. Whoever had broken into my shop was almost certainly the same person sending threatening cards, flowers, etc. My anonymous phone caller was someone I knew or someone who had access to the phone directory of someone I knew, namely Robert.

That all added up, right? Logically, Robert's killer and my stalker had to be one and the same.

And while I was the one who had originally suggested the possibility of a serial killer — and as popular as barking mad, opera-playing, Chianti-swilling serial killers are in fiction — I was more and more inclined to believe that whoever had killed Robert had some discernable motive.

I was thinking aloud, "He lets himself in with Robert's key. He trashes my place, leaves the cat in the trunk to rot and lets himself out again. Why didn't he just wait and kill me?"

Riordan traced the painted leaf on the cup with his thumb. "Harassment? Dirty tricks? Maybe someone who knows you've got a bum ticker."

"You think someone's trying to scare me to death?"

Riordan shrugged.

"Why not just kill me?" I repeated.

"I'll play. Why not?"

As they used to say in those B sci-fi movies from the Fifties: Reverse polarization! What was the motive for *not* killing me?

I rose, refilled my cup. "Was the same weapon used to kill Claude and Robert?"

"Won't know for sure till we see the ME's report. I'd guess yes. I'm not big on coincidence. I'll tell you something, though. The wounds were not the same. The level of rage was not there."

I remembered how the newspapers had described the viciousness with which Robert had been attacked. His face slashed, stab wounds in his throat, his eyes —

"Claude was killed more...conventionally?"

He smiled faintly. "You could put it that way. Hersey's killer was acting out some fantasy. An orgy of violence. La Pierra's was in a hurry."

"He couldn't have known I was coming back."

"Right."

"Unless you think I killed Claude?"

He glanced at the slightly puffy knuckles of my hand resting on the table. "Not nearly enough blood on your clothes. And no murder weapon."

"Not even in the Bronco?" I inquired blandly. "I wondered why you were so considerate as to have me driven home."

"You're so cynical." Riordan was grinning.

He drained his cup. Rose to leave. I rose too and went to get his jacket. Brown leather and no epaulettes. So maybe the S/M thing was more of a hobby than a vocation.

At the door I asked, "Have you had any luck tracing Felice or any of the others from the Chess Club?"

He shrugged into his jacket, not meeting my eyes. "No."

"No. You haven't even tried."

I must have sounded bitter enough that he said after a moment, "Look, I did run some inquiries. Okay? Nothing yet."

* * * * *

Friday afternoon brought galleys from my publisher. This proof that my first novel was fast approaching the reality stage took my mind off my other problems. I went upstairs, made myself a cup of Special Roast, got out a box of Belgian chocolate almond cookies, and began poring over the galleys. Soon I was lost again in the world of my own imagination, wincing at certain phrases, pleasantly surprised at others. Absorbed in the pages before me, I was amazed when I came up for air and it was nearly five o'clock.

I went downstairs. Angus was eating a subway sandwich and pondering the obituary section of the *Times*. Bits of lettuce and salami dotted the newsprint like confetti.

"Dead you wail the western male," he enunciated through layers of sandwich.

"Come again?" Not that anything surprised me at this point. If he'd started spouting Chaucer I'd have taken it as par for the course.

Angus masticated ferociously, swallowed, and repeated as though for the deaf, "Did you want the rest of the mail?"

"Thank you. I did." I picked up the bundle of mail and felt around under the counter. "Do you know what happened to the letter opener?"

"No."

"It was right here." I squatted down, running my hands along the shelves. "It looks like a miniature dagger. Mother of Pearl handle?"

Actually it was a witch's bolline, a long ago Halloween gag gift from Mel.

"I never saw it," said Angus.

I stared at him. He blinked nervously behind his specs, bit his lip. I had no idea if he was lying or not. He was the kind of kid who acts guilty even when he isn't.

I tried to think of the last time I'd seen the letter opener. I'd been using the one in my office for the past few days. I didn't remember seeing the bolline since Robert had opened the mail Friday last.

It wasn't like I still had any special attachment to the thing. I couldn't rid myself of the suspicion it had been taken during last Monday's break-in, but that didn't make sense. Still, the feeling of unease persisted.

I went back to the office and began shuffling through the post. Along with the usual books and magazines and catalogs (how did I get on the *Things You Never Knew Existed* mailing list?) was a flat, square package wrapped in brown paper and tied with string. The writing was crooked, a child's scrawl in red crayon.

I used my pen knife on the string. Slid the blade beneath the brown flaps. A CD lay on my desk. Verdi's *Requiem*.

"God damn it!" I picked the plastic case up and threw it across the room. The case pinwheeled through the air, hit the metal shelf and broke open. Two parts landed on the floor. The CD rolled in a neat circle, flipped over and lay face up.

I jumped up, crossed the room in two strides and picked up the CD. Across the front in black Sharpie were printed the words, *"Our fatal shadows that walk by us still."*

Fatal shadows. Fatal shit. I reached for the phone.

But then, slowly, I replaced the receiver. What was the point in calling the police? Messrs. Serve and Protect had me pegged as a hysterical faggot who had only himself to blame if a disgruntled suitor was stalking him. Riordan was obviously undecided as to whether I was capable of sending myself gruesome presents for attention. Not amazing if he still suspected me of offing Robert.

I went upstairs, put the CD on the player. Immediately the music spilled out, silken and somber, gliding around the sunlit rooms, trailing after me into my study. I pulled out my *Bartlett's Familiar Quotations* and scanned the index. I found what I was looking for under "Fatal." English Dramatist John Fletcher (1579-1625) — of whom I'd never heard — had written something called "Honest Man's Fortune."

Man is his own star; and the soul that can
Render an honest and perfect man,
Commands all light, all influence, all fate,
Nothing to him falls early or too late.
Our acts, our angels are, for good or ill
Our fatal shadows that walk by us still.

CHAPTER TWELVE

What would Grace Latham have done in my position? Well, in close to twenty mystery novels she would have run straight to the murderer with the only piece of proof, and placed herself in mortal jeopardy. That was the difference between me and Grace — she usually managed to stumble onto a piece of evidence, a useful clue, *something*. Grace also had dapper Colonel Primrose to feed her inside info and to save her well-bred ass at the last minute. I had no such ally.

So despite the blue skies smiling at me that early Saturday morning, my mood was gloomy. I stood at the kitchen window watching white clouds gambol playfully across blue fields of sky, the sun shining with relentless cheer, drying out the rain puddles, the wet roofs, the glistening streets — and my soggy brain.

Over a can of Tab I jotted down what I thought I knew so far — what I believed to be the facts of the case.

Tara had motive: according to the police she stood to inherit a sizeable chunk of change. That was usually sufficient grounds for murder in most Leslie Ford novels, but how did it apply to knocking me off? I didn't benefit from Robert's will, and when I died whatever I left went to various gay men's organizations.

I could think of other reasons someone might decide to get rid of Robert: jealousy, for one. Claude had been sick with jealousy after Robert dumped him, but Claude had been killed too. Of course Claude was just one of many, so maybe another of Robert's discarded lovers was out there evening the score. But again, why come after me? Robert and I had not been romantically involved.

Maybe Robert *had* been the victim of a hate crime. Max certainly loathed Robert, but I couldn't quite picture Max killing Robert except in the heat of the moment. Robert's murder had been premeditated. No one randomly carries chess pieces around, except maybe disgruntled Russian ex-champs. Besides, while Max might not care for my lifestyle — or me, for that matter — I couldn't believe my existence troubled him enough for him to bother killing me.

I scratched my nose with the end of my pen. Yeah, lots of possible reasons, and each more improbable than the last. Maybe the blackmail theory wasn't so far-fetched. Rob desperately needed money and he would get a kick out of watching someone squirm. He'd never had any sense about taking a joke too far. And Detective Riordan, for example, didn't seem to enjoy much sense of humor. But while I could see it might be to Riordan's advantage to frame me for Robert's murder, I couldn't see him risking a third homicide.

So while I could think of a number of reasons — bad and good — for killing Robert, I couldn't arrive at a common motive for eliminating both Robert and me. And I was convinced that Robert's murder was not a unique and separate event. It was connected to … my murder.

Though apparently the cops didn't share my vision, I believed this indicated a larger pattern. But that's where my tidy logical equation fell apart. Why hadn't I been killed? Why instead had Claude been killed? What did Claude have to do with anything?

I sighed and tossed my pen down. Went to put on Verdi's *Requiem* once more. Though it had probably been intended to strike terror in my heart, ironically, as I listened absently to the haunting beauty of "Libera Me" I felt calm, certain that if I just kept at it, the answer would come to me. So what if the police wouldn't help me? The police didn't have a vested interest. I did.

The problem was, I kind of had to agree with Riordan and the inscrutable Chan. A motive for murder stretching back to adolescence seemed farfetched.

What the hell did it mean? That I could add the facts of the case all day, and not get any closer to the truth?

I glanced at the clock, got out the phone book and tried calling all the numbers under "Landis." As it was Saturday I hit fewer answering machines and more real people, but eight phone calls later I still had no leads. I didn't get it. It always worked in mystery novels.

Right before eleven o'clock I went downstairs to spell Angus. He was reading about Claude's murder in the paper which he folded guiltily and shoved beneath the counter when I appeared. I'd already caught the headline, "Slasher Targets Gay Community."

We had a writer's signing scheduled for the next weekend — provided we were all still alive for it. A lot of preparation goes into a successful signing: having enough of the author's books on hand, advertising ahead of time, planning the refreshments. I put as much time into it as I hoped someone would do for me one day.

Since this author was gay, I knew we'd have to prep harder than usual. Claude had been lined up to handle the refreshments; now it was back to me and Trader Joe's.

Angus returned from lunch and we worked out the menu; which is to say, I threw ideas out and Angus made faces and simulated gagging motions.

"Cheese puffs," he advised.

"Powdered cheese gets all over the books."

"Everybody loves cheesy puffs. Even f —"

"Even fags?"

He started coughing as though he'd inhaled one of his own cheesy puffs.

I eyed him. "From your vast culinary expertise what do you think about water chestnuts wrapped in bacon?"

"Uh … yeah, whatever. I mean. …"

I waited.

Angus fiddled with a paper clip. "Do you need me that day?"

"Some reason you don't want to be here?"

Angus turned red everywhere his skin showed and I felt a little sorry for him.

"No," he squeaked.

"Good. Because I need you here."

"It's just — it's a full moon."

I bit back my first comment and said, "There will be other full moons, Angus."

* * * * *

Bruce called a couple of hours later. I was doing the bills. Not my favorite thing.

"What are you doing?" His voice was low, intimate.

"Working."

Quiet laugh. "Doing what?"

"The usual. What are you doing? What are you working on these days?" Two phone calls in less than twelve hours. Wow. At long last I was winning friends and influencing people.

"I'm freelance. I pick and choose." He talked about what he was picking and choosing. I listened absently, totting figures. "I don't like to travel though," Bruce was saying. "I must be getting old. I try to find stuff that interests me close to home."

"Must be nice." I squinted at my calculations.

A pause and then, "Is something wrong?"

"No. Of course not."

"Yeah. Something is. Look, Adrien, I told you the truth. I'm not working on this Gay Slasher story. *Boytimes* put a staffer on it. I just want to see you again."

"I believe you."

"So when can I see you?"

I don't know what the problem was. I'd been celibate — which is a more dignified word for lonely — for years. Now I had someone in my life saying all the right things, doing all the right things, and suddenly I felt pressured. So much for preaching to Riordan about healthy, satisfying, homosexual relationships.

"I don't know," I said finally.

"Tonight?"

I tried to think of a good reason not to. There wasn't one.

"Tonight is fine."

"I'll pick you up."

* * * * *

Late afternoon trade picked up and I had to put aside the amateur sleuthing for the day.

After an initially slow start, business was improving steadily. That was one reason I had been able to offer Robert a job when he needed one — the store was really more than I could handle on my own — although I had tried. I had been reluctant to end my period of suspended animation by letting a living breathing person invade my space. Now I couldn't help feeling like maybe that instinct had been a good one.

When we finally had a lull, I took a quick break, eating an apple and half a chicken salad sandwich in my office while I thumbed once more through Robert's yearbook. I studied the immature, unformed faces of the Chess Club as though it would be possible to read their thoughts. That's when the light bulb went on.

Tara.

No, she hadn't belonged to the Chess Club. No, she hadn't even attended West Valley Academy till the following year, but she had spent that long hot summer with Robert, and she had been eager to know everything about him. And Robert had liked to talk.

I dialed Tara.

She wasn't thrilled to hear from me. I could hear a TV blasting and kids yelling in the background. Sioux City Serenade.

"Adrien, it was a long time ago," Tara protested finally when I'd explained what I was after.

"I know, but try to remember. The Chess Club broke up after one semester. Why?"

"It's a boring game."

"Come on, Tara."

A heavy sigh all along the miles of corn fields and rolling prairie.

"I don't really know. That's the truth."

"What did Robert say?"

I could hear her hesitation, her doubt. "If he'd wanted you to know, Adrien, he'd have told you."

"Oh for — !"

Irritably, she said, "Somebody cheated, I think. There was this big match. Tournament, I guess you'd call it, between all these schools. Someone from West Valley cheated. West Valley was disqualified."

I absorbed this doubtfully. "That can't be it." I don't know what I was expecting. Yes, I do. Reason for murder.

"Well, that's the only thing I know of. Think about it, Adrien. It was very embarrassing. Kids don't like to be embarrassed. Especially teenagers. Robert was still fuming months later."

Robert did not like to be embarrassed, that had never changed. He did not like to seem foolish. He did not like to appear in the wrong. But Robert had not cheated. He would never cheat in a million years — and Robert was the one who was dead.

I tried to remember, but my perceptions of that year were colored by the two main events of my life up to that point: nearly dying, and realizing I was gay. The two had seemed inextricably linked.

"Who cheated?"

"Bob never said."

"Come off it, Tara. Rob told you everything."

"Not everything," she said bitterly and covered the mouthpiece to snap at one of the kids.

This reminded me of something that had been nagging at me. "Tara, why were you in L.A. before Robert was killed?"

Her breath caught sharply. "How do you know that?"

"Robert told me."

"Bob didn't —" she broke off and said, "I've got to go."

Huh? "Wait! One more question, please, Tara. Why did the Chess Club fall apart?"

"Mr. Atkins, the sponsor, pulled the plug."

"Why?"

"I guess because of the cheating incident. I don't know. Look, Adrien, you'd better not be sticking your nose in my personal life."

"I'm not. Why did Atkins pull the plug?"

"Well, Nancy Drew, why don't you ask him?" she said and hung up.

CHAPTER THIRTEEN

Mr. Atkins had retired from the thankless task of trying to force-feed knowledge to children who now packed guns. The Head Master's secretary took my name and number and promised to pass them along.

I went downstairs and freed Angus from the shackles of slavery — you would have thought so anyway from the way he hightailed it. I locked up.

As I started up the staircase I thought I heard a soft rustling from the rear of the shop.

I went back downstairs, walked down the narrow aisles through the towering paperback canyons. Allingham to Zubro, there was nothing out of order. I poked my head in the office.

"Hello?"

Nothing.

Feeling silly I snapped the light off again and went upstairs to dress for meeting Bruce.

I had a drink while I shaved. I spent a long time trying to decide what to wear, settling on a dress shirt in a shade the sales associate at Saks called "curry," and a pair of black trousers. I felt ridiculously nervous. When the phone rang I snatched it off the receiver.

It was Detective Riordan and he sounded grim. "Two things: we just got the paperwork from Buffalo PD. Richard Corday died from injuries sustained falling twelve stories onto a cement poolyard."

I swallowed hard. "Was it suicide?"

"It was a suspicious death. Corday checked in alone, and only his personal effects were found in the room; but one of the maids said she had accidentally walked in on Corday and a guest a few hours earlier."

"A man?"

"A woman, she thought. She saw women's clothes tossed around the room."

"That's impossible."

"I'm just giving you the facts."

"Wait a minute." I was thinking out loud. "Suppose the women's clothes were Rusty's? He died in drag."

Silence. "It's a possibility," he said grudgingly.

"Could he have fallen accidentally?"

"No way. They faxed over photos of the room, including the windows. He could have jumped or he could have been stuffed out, but he couldn't have lost his balance. He was drunk however, and he was wearing women's clothing, which sounded enough like reason for suicide to the boys in Buffalo."

"Was there a chess piece anywhere?"

"I was getting to that. In Corday's color-coordinated handbag were his American Express card —"

"Don't leave home without it," I murmured.

"His keys — including his room key, a clean white hanky, a MAC lipstick — Pink Glaze, if you're interested, and one chess piece. A queen."

Never had I felt so little pleasure in being right.

Could Rusty's death be unconnected? After all, he didn't even live in the same state.

But then what about the coincidence of his belonging to the Chess Club? The Chess Club had to play into it — how else could one explain a game piece clutched in a dying man's hand? There was no chess set in Robert's apartment that I'd noticed. His killer had to have left it as a calling card.

I said, "You told me Tara was in L.A. when Robert died. Do you know why?"

"To get back with him."

"She told me Robert didn't know she was here."

"She was here to ask his family to pull an intervention."

"An *intervention?* What were they going to intervene with? His being gay?"

"That's the story."

"And you believe it?"

"Hersey's sisters corroborated her story."

I started as I heard the downstairs buzzer. Bruce was early.

"You still there?" Riordan asked.

"Hmm? Yes, I'm here. You said two things."

"Second thing. Remind your mother," his voice crackled with hostility, "and her mouthpiece that you have been handled with kid gloves up until now. We could have hauled your bony ass in for interrogation anytime we chose. We haven't done that, have we?"

"No." I was barely able to form the word.

"No. In fact, I went out of my way to keep you off ice. And that was before I knew Mommy Dearest and the police chief's wife are on the same Save-the-Spaniels committee. I don't appreciate getting called on the carpet. Got that?"

I could feel myself turning into an ice sculpture: the chilling effect of humiliation. Before I could explain, Riordan's voice altered, grew brisk, impersonal. I knew someone was standing near him. "I've got to go."

He rang off and I went downstairs to meet Bruce.

* * * * *

We dined at Celestino on the patio. It was crowded and chilly. People talked and smoked at other tables, but even after a couple of drinks I felt removed from my surroundings, detached. I blamed it on Riordan's phone call and tried to shake off my preoccupation.

Over swordfish carpaccio with orange and fennel salad, I got Bruce to tell me about himself. Used to doing the interviewing, he was clearly not comfortable on this side of the questions, but I'd had enough of my own problems for a while. I kept turning the conversation back to Bruce, and gradually, soup through dessert, I got his life story. Like me he'd grown up in the Valley. Unlike me he'd attended public schools, graduating from Chatsworth High and going on to CSUN. Like me, he'd realized he was gay his last year of high school. Unlike me, his family had disowned him the minute he came out of the closet.

"In retrospect it would have been wiser to wait, like you did, to break it to them."

"It wasn't wisdom," I told him. "My motto growing up was always, 'Discretion is the better part of valor.'"

He said reflectively, "I think they would have come to terms with it, but both my parents died right after I graduated from college."

"I'm sorry."

He smiled awkwardly. "Your family was more enlightened, I take it?"

I shrugged. "In a weird way I think my mother is relieved there will never be a young Mrs. English to contend with. She's not keen on competition." I grinned wryly meeting Bruce's sympathetic gaze.

He didn't talk much about his work, seeming reticent, as though he suspected I might not approve. I tried to make all the appropriate noises and faces. I realized though that I was trying too hard.

Bruce realized it too. "I'm boring you, aren't I?"

"Hell no!"

His lopsided smile was rueful and appealing in his homely face. "It's okay. I bore myself."

"No, Bruce. I've just got a lot on my mind."

"Were you lovers?"

"Who?"

"You and Hersey."

"No. A long time ago." I didn't want to talk about it. I had to work through those memories on my own.

"What about you and — what was his name? Pierre?"

"La Pierra. No. He was … ." I took a breath. "A good friend. I should have —"

"What?" His solemn dark eyes were curious.

I shook my head. I didn't want to share those thoughts either — maybe not the most promising indicator of a change in my emotional litmus. I put my hand over my glass when he raised the wine bottle. He frowned. "What's the problem?"

"Two of my closest friends have been killed."

"Do you think there's a connection?"

"Of course there's a connection."

"I mean to you."

"Me?"

He nodded gravely. "Was there anything else they had in common?"

I looked at him, but I was seeing Robert. What did Robert and I have in common?

We were both gay. We were the same age and race. We went to the same high school. We belonged to the Chess Club in high school — as well as the tennis team and sharing many of the same classes. We both knew Claude. We both knew Tara. We both knew a lot of the same people. So what?

The truth was, Robert and I had very little in common besides being gay and going to high school together.

Into my silence, Bruce said softly, "There is something, isn't there?"

I barely heard him. Had Claude hedged about knowing who Robert was seeing before his death? Maybe he really hadn't known. Whoever Robert had been seeing it hadn't been for long or openly, because none of Robert's crowd knew anything about the guy. Claude had claimed Riordan had killed Robert. Claude had claimed Riordan was going to kill him.

Something didn't make sense. Should I assume that Robert's killer and Claude's killer were the same? Did that only hold true if Robert's killer and my stalker were the same? Why kill Claude? Why not kill me?

Were the flowers and CD a prelude to murder? Had Robert also received these tokens of esteem? If so, he hadn't considered himself "stalked." Maybe I was more insecure.

Robert had not been stalked. Claude had not been stalked. But Claude and Robert were both dead. I was being stalked but I was not dead. Not yet.

I became aware that Bruce was waiting for an answer. I said, "You probably know more about that than me."

"I'm off the story, remember? Conflict of interest."

I wondered if he resented that conflict? How much did his career mean to him? How far could he be trusted?"

"Do you play chess?" I asked suddenly.

He smiled. "Sure. You?"

"Not for years. I was thinking — if there's some special significance to chess."

"Like what?"

"I don't know." I sighed. Ran a hand through my hair. I was tired. And once again I'd had too much to drink.

"There's something you're not telling me," Bruce's gaze held mine.

"It's just a theory."

"Tell me."

Belatedly, I remembered Riordan had warned me to keep my mouth shut. "No. It's nothing." I looked at my watch. Tried not to yawn.

"Did you want to get out of here, Adrien?" he asked abruptly.

* * * * *

It was just a couple of minutes drive back to the bookstore.

"I had this planned so differently," Bruce said in the quiet of the car.

"I had a good time."

In the silence that stretched, he asked diffidently, "Will you come back to my place?"

We drove back to Bruce's. He lived in one of those quiet Chatsworth neighborhoods in one of those sprawling brown-and-yellow ranch-style houses. The grass was getting long, there were dandelions in the flower beds, and the asphalt driveway needed resurfacing.

Bruce let us into the dark house. My nostrils twitched at the faint scent of air freshener and cat.

"Sorry it's such a mess." He switched on the lights as we went through the rooms.

It wasn't a mess. It was spotless. It also wasn't like anything I'd imagined. Plastic fruit in bowls, the Leaning Tree gallery of Indian paintings, a bookshelf full of stuff like Dr. Spock on raising kids, Barbara Cartland romances, an out of date set of *Encyclopedia Britannica*. The china cabinet was full of pink stemware. The kind of stuff you get at markets for buying so many dollars worth of produce. It didn't strike me as Bruce's taste.

"Did you want a glass of wine?"

May as well be drunk as the way I am, I thought. "Sure."

There were plenty of those multi-picture frames featuring a nice middle-class American family, mom and dad and a cute little girl who went from pigtails to wedding gown. There were even photos of assorted dogs and cats, but no photos of Bruce. Pale squares and ovals on the wall indicated where his pictures once hung.

"This was your Mom and Dad's house?" I lifted up a figurine. A dog tugging on a girl's dress.

"Yeah. I'm not here enough to bother clearing this junk out," Bruce explained, again reading my thoughts. He brought me a glass of wine.

We touched glasses and Bruce kissed me.

* * * * *

Moonlight flooded the room but Bruce slept peacefully on. I eased gingerly out from under his arm, padded over to the window, put one hand on the cool glass.

The backyard was vaguely familiar like so many yards out of my Southern California childhood. There was a cactus garden in the center of the patio, which featured a built-in barbecue. In the jungle of weeds stood a rusted swing set, gilded in moonlight. I could make out the roof of an empty dog house behind tufts of dead ornamental grass. And, unless I missed my guess, around the corner of the house would be a narrow walkway with steps leading up to a side door. Potted palms on either side.

"What are you thinking about?" Bruce's whisper behind me had me starting. He put a hand on my shoulder, warm, possessive.

"Nothing."

"More bad dreams?" His voice was as low as though he feared his parents could still hear.

I shook my head.

He kissed my shoulder. "You're so beautiful."

There was a sudden blockage in my throat. "Bruce —"

"You don't know how long I've dreamed of you here. With me. Like this." He guided me back to bed.

We lay down, put our arms around each other. Already this was becoming familiar.

I wanted it to be familiar. I wanted it to be right. I rejected the disloyal thought that Bruce was clutching me too tightly, that his urgent gasps didn't leave me room to breathe, that he was rough when I needed tenderness, and tentative when I needed sureness.

"Tell me what you're thinking."

"I'm not thinking."

"I love you," Bruce murmured against my ear. I turned my head quickly, stopping his words with my kiss.

* * * * *

The answering machine was signaling disaster when I finally got in. Some impulse made me hit Play despite my exhaustion.

"Where the hell are you?" Riordan sounded ... angry wasn't quite the word. "Call me when you get in. I don't care what time it is." He recited a couple of new numbers to phone.

I didn't think he meant five-thirty in the morning, and I didn't have the energy to deal with him right now anyway. I stripped, dived into bed, loving the cool kiss of my own sheets on my nakedness. The bed did a spin. I closed my eyes. Passed out.

* * * * *

I was surprised when Mr. Atkins called. He said he always enjoyed meeting with former students, and we arranged to meet for lunch at the Denny's on Topanga Canyon.

I recognized him immediately in blue-tinted spectacles that matched a baggy sleeveless sweater. I recalled that he had a sleeveless sweater in every shade of blue. His hair was thinning but still longish. It occurred to me that while he had seemed ancient and venerable to my 11th grader eyes, he couldn't have been that old. He was only about sixty now.

"I come here for the early bird specials," he informed me with a wink, and poured a second packet of C&H into his tea. "That's the beauty of early retirement, son. You're still young enough to enjoy life."

We ordered, and while we waited to be served Mr. Atkins said, "I was very sorry to hear about Robert Hersey. I told my wife when I read the story in the paper what a waste it was. Such a bright, handsome kid."

"This may sound crazy," I said, rearranging the salt shakers. "But I'm afraid Robert's death could have something to do with what happened with the Chess Club."

"You've got to be kidding." Mr. Atkins pushed his glasses back up his nose and frowned at me.

"No. Rusty Corday's dead too — also under suspicious circumstances. Both Rusty and Rob were found with … well … chess pieces."

"What do you mean "found" with them?"

I explained what I meant. Mr. Atkins' eyebrows shot up. "Well of course the whole school knew about Corday, but Hersey. I just can't believe that. Hersey a queer?" He considered me, and I saw the light dawn. "Ah, I see," he said regretfully.

Maybe at some point that doesn't sting any more. I said stiffly, "The thing is, two people dead out of such a small group seems like too much of a coincidence."

"Don't get me wrong, son," Mr. Atkins said. "Moralizing went out with Henry James. But it's an unhealthy way to live, isn't it?"

There were a number of responses to that. None conducive to getting more information.

The waitress brought our lunches. As soon as she was out of range, Mr. Atkins said, "I think you're wrong, though. I admit at the time there might have been reason for murder, if you listen to the talk show hosts. There's nothing more unstable than the adolescent male."

"What actually happened?"

"You were there. Oh, that's right. You came down with mono or something, didn't you?"

"When I got back you had quit sponsoring the club."

"Hell. I should hope so. What a mess!" He shook his head and ate a french fry. "Well, it's no mystery. We were invited to the All City Tournament, and Grant Landis, the big doofus, cheated. Tried to cheat anyway. Knocked the board after making an illegal move or some such crap. You can't cheat at chess. Not like that."

"What happened?"

"We were disqualified." He made a face. "The kids were humiliated and angry. Landis was — well, I felt sorry for the kid. Poor bastard. All he wanted was to fit in. You know the kind of kid who tries too hard to be funny. Gets a laugh and then keeps telling the same joke over and over. He had a knack for irritating and annoying the kids he most wanted to impress — like your pal Hersey."

I tried to remember Landis. I thought maybe Rob and I had gone over to his house once or twice for study groups, but I couldn't put a face to the name. Dark, I thought. Bushy dark hair when nobody was wearing bushy dark hair. Glasses, maybe.

"And you quit sponsoring the club? Why not just throw Landis out?"

"He quit." Mr. Atkins looked uncomfortable at some memory. "Kids are merciless. One of the pack shows weakness and the others'll devour him."

"And that was it? They drove Landis out and you quit sponsoring the club?"

Mr. Atkins ate another french fry.

"There's something else, isn't there? Can't you tell me? It might be important."

"It was a long time ago, son." He chewed thoughtfully.

"What happened to Landis? I don't remember him my senior year."

"Transferred out. Public school." Behind the blue shades his eyes met mine and flicked away.

I said, "Mr. Atkins, it's not curiosity. I've got to know."

Mr. Atkins finished chewing and seemed to come to some conclusion.

"Suit yourself. About a month after the whole fiasco Landis was jumped one night coming home from the library. Well, Landis was a strapping kid. Skinny but substantial. So there had to be a gang of them. Anyway, they held him down, shaved his entire body, smeared make up all over his face, and put him in a dress. Then the little shits took photos which they handed round the school."

I was silent trying to imagine this.

"Of course there was a stink to high heaven. We had everyone from the cops to the school board breathing down our neck. But nobody ever squealed."

"Landis must have known who did it."

"He said they wore masks. Maybe they did, but I always thought he was lying. I think he knew who it was, but what the hell. It wouldn't have made his life any easier to finger them." He added caustically, "Nowadays he'd have just come back with an automatic weapon."

"Why did you assume it was somebody in the Chess Club? It sounds more like something a bunch of asshole jocks would do."

"The Chess Club *was* a bunch of asshole jocks," Mr. Atkins retorted. "Hersey was on the tennis team. So were you for that matter. Felicity, or whatever her name was, was the shining star of women's softball. And Andrew Chin was a diver."

"What about Rusty Corday?"

"Corday? Was he the wispy little red-haired queer bait?" He caught my eyes. "Sorry, but the kid was flaming."

I was silent. I had to give old Mr. Chips credit. I'd never have dreamed he was so full of biases back in the days of chalkboards and report cards. He'd seemed the epitome of the open-minded nonjudgmental educator.

I said slowly, thinking aloud. "Rob, Rusty and I were all gay. Not that Rob and I would have called it *that*, even to each other. Not then. Although what the hell we thought we were doing …."

Mr. Atkins cleared his throat uneasily, recalling me to the present.

"Was Landis gay? Or Chin?" I asked.

"Kids that age don't know what they are."

"But they dressed Landis in drag?"

"That doesn't prove he was queer."

"That could have been the message though. Maybe it was an accusation aimed at the entire club."

"No."

"You seem pretty sure."

"You teach a few years and you get an ear for lies. I don't know who, and I don't know why, but it was the kids in the Chess Club that humiliated Landis that way. The photos were developed in the journalism class."

Robert.

I began to understand why Robert had sort of forgot to mention any of this to me during the long months of my convalescence. He'd had a tendency even then to resent "Tiny Tim's lectures."

Mr. Atkins finished his french fries. "All the same, son, I think you're reaching. I don't believe there could be any connection between Hersey's death and the Chess Club."

"Why's that?"

"The one with the — er — motive would be Landis. Right? Well Landis is dead. He died right after high school."

CHAPTER FOURTEEN

"**I** need to see you tonight," Bruce's voice said on my answering machine.

I fast forwarded through the rest of his message. A lot of tape.

Three hang ups and then Riordan, terse and to the point. "Call me when you get in."

I called the Hollywood Investigative Services Unit and asked for Homicide. After a couple of transfers I got Prince Charming himself.

"Yeah? Riordan here."

"It's me. Adrien," I said ungrammatically.

"Where the *hell* —" There was a pause. Then, "Hang on a sec." I was back on hold. A couple of minutes later Riordan came back on the line. "Still there?"

"What are you doing, tracing my call? I'm at home."

"I told you to call me last night."

"I wasn't home last night. I left a message for you this morning."

"Just shut up and listen."

"Well since you ask so nicely … ."

There was silence. I listened. He didn't say anything.

"Are we communicating through the Psychic Hotline or what?"

"Shut up a sec," he said from between his pearly whites.

I shut up. Welcome to the closet, I thought. Is it dark in here or is it just me?

Riordan said very quietly, "Listen, I don't want you to overreact, but I think you may be...next."

"What?" I guess it was the uncharacteristically subdued way he spoke. It scared the hell out of me. "I *told* you!"

"Yes. I owe you an apology. Well, sort of."

"You got that right." Though it was what I'd been yelping about all along, it suddenly seemed preposterous. "What makes you think I'm...next?"

"It's this frigging Chess Club thing. I spent the last forty-eight hours checking into it."

"And?"

"They're all dead."

That hit home like a punch to the solar plexus. I managed, "All of them? They're *all* dead?"

"All but you, buddy boy."

I closed my eyes. "How?"

"Landis committed suicide."

"Right after graduation. I know."

"Andrew Chin died in a car accident three years ago. The brakes failed on his BMW."

"And Corday shuffled off to Buffalo."

"Uh huh, but the clincher is Burns. Two years ago Dr. Felice Burns was stabbed to death in the hospital parking lot where she worked."

I sucked in a sharp breath. "Then why did no one connect it?"

"There was nothing to connect at the time. Besides, Burns died out of state. She lived in Seattle."

Riordan had managed to gather a lot of information fast. Either he had connections or he had pulled in favors. I said slowly, "But the MO keeps changing: stabbing, cutting brake lines —"

"How do you know Chin's brake lines were cut?"

"Because I cut them! Jesus, I assumed, okay?"

"God save me from amateurs."

I allowed myself one sweet moment of satisfaction. "You're just pissed because you were wrong and I was right."

"And I have to live with it for the rest of my life." He sounded sarcastic, not sorry.

"So how was Andy murdered?"

"I didn't say he was murdered. As a matter of fact, from everything we can find out, it looks like it really was just an accident."

"I don't believe that."

"I hate to disappoint you, but accidents do happen."

"Yeah, mostly within five miles of home. You don't think Felice was accidentally stabbed to death, do you?"

He sounded like someone struggling for patience. "Obviously *she* was murdered. Obviously I think the odds are against coincidence. But I have to tell you, there was no chess piece found on Chin's body or in his personal effects."

"Maybe they missed it."

"That's not the kind of thing that gets missed in an investigation." His tone had become chilly at this implied inefficiency of brother law enforcement.

"So what are you saying? You *don't* think there's a connection?"

"Ease up, English. There *was* a chess piece found in Felice Burns' purse. A black knight."

"Why a knight? Why black?"

"My guess? She was African-American. Black. Secondly, she was not a queen. She was not even a lesbian. She was a happily married pediatrician with a kid of her own. Maybe the horse symbolizes something? Maybe it's an insult. She was a good ride? I don't know how some sick bastard might reason."

"It doesn't make sense. If everyone's dead, who's doing this?" I filled him in on what I had learned from Mr. Atkins.

When I had finally run to a stop in the face of his daunting silence he said very mildly, "Not too bad for an amateur, English. I'll give you that. Now listen to me very carefully. I will take it from here. You keep your god-damned nose out of it. Is that clear? Do I make myself understood?"

Not that I had any idea of how to proceed even if I wanted to, but I heard myself say, "Sorry? I'm next on the Hit Parade, remember?"

"That's right. I'm sharing information that I could get my ass canned for sharing so that you can protect yourself, not so that you can play amateur sleuth like some character in your book."

"And how am I supposed to protect myself?"

"By letting the police do their job."

I heard the edge in my laugh and knew he did too. "Yeah, right. Twenty-four hours ago the police thought I was a hysterical faggot making this up, if not actually a murderer. Sorry if I don't have a lot of faith in the p —"

He interrupted, "I said I was sorry. Okay? That's a murder investigation. Feelings get hurt. Hell, why am I explaining?"

I sure didn't know. Into my silence he said more reasonably, "I believe we're dealing with a possible serial killer. I believe you could be targeted. That's just my gut. I have yet to convince my superiors of this. Chin's death doesn't fit and neither does La Pierra's."

"So what are you saying?"

"I'm saying that we need to follow procedure in order to nail this guy. See — we don't actually have a suspect."

Me. I was the only suspect still standing. Reading between the lines, I grasped what Riordan was actually saying. Since the departmental view was that I probably was the killer, they weren't going to expend a lot of energy on protecting me.

"What you're saying is, no one is going to take this seriously until they find me carved up in an alley."

"I'm saying — I'm saying you need to be careful."

"I can't stay locked up twenty-four hours a day! I can't even leave town because he travels, right? He found Rusty in Buffalo. Felice in Seattle."

"Do you have a gun?"

"Me? No."

"That's probably just as well," he said dryly. "Okay, do you have someone you can stay with? Hell, stay with your mother. The Pentagon doesn't have the security system she's got."

I really *would* rather die. "I'm not putting my mother in the path of a serial killer. Thanks for the thought."

"God help the serial killer who tackles your mother," Riordan muttered. "Listen, just use common sense. Your friends had no warning. You do. If you're by yourself, keep the doors locked and have a phone handy. Avoid alleys."

"Thanks," I said sourly.

"I'll have a squad car swing by every couple of hours. How's that?"

"Great."

"And don't go anywhere without letting me know. I mean *anywhere*."

"Wow," I blurted. "It's like we're going steady. How long am I under house arrest?"

It was the loudest silence I'd ever heard. No sense of humor, this lawman.

He said finally, very reasonably, "I have a lead. Nothing solid yet. I'll let you know how it turns out. Fair enough?"

"Hell no."

He smothered a laugh. "You'll be fine. But if you see or hear anything suspicious, dial 911."

* * * * *

The rest of the day passed uneventfully; yet I felt increasingly keyed-up, strained. Despite the Technicolor azure skies the air felt snappish, like right before a storm. Late afternoon the wind picked up. The old building creaked and muttered. I concurred.

I found the bolline in my office desk drawer — where it had never been before. So much for my theory it had been taken during the break-in. Angus avoided my eyes when I mentioned I'd found it. I let him go early and locked the door after him. I drew the security bars across. Watched him walk to his car.

But the minute Angus's Volkswagen buzzed out of the lot I became uneasy, looking over my shoulder at every creak in the timbers, starting when I caught a glimpse of my own reflection in the oval mirror over the fireplace. It could take years to catch this maniac. Look at the Zodiac killer. Look at all those people on *Unsolved Mysteries*.

Why come after me? I protested mentally. I wasn't even there! I wouldn't have gone along with the public humiliation of Landis. But maybe my stalker was someone who didn't know that I hadn't been there. Or maybe he didn't care because he had grown to like killing people. Or maybe he was a freaking nutcase and the rules of sanity didn't apply.

I thought of Mr. Atkins and his view of "emotionally unstable adolescent males." I considered the thing that had happened to Landis. It was horrible and cruel. I hated thinking Rob had been part of that, and yet I believed it. It was the kind of thing he deeply regretted as an adult. He didn't like hurting people; it just seemed to come naturally to him.

And what about poor Landis? Kids felt everything intensely. They reacted intensely. Had he lived, he probably would have put that night in perspective. Not that the wounds of adolescence couldn't still hurt. I thought about Bruce's parents and their rejection. And I can still remember my mother saying sadly, "Your father would be *so* disappointed in you, Adrien." I don't remember what it was over, just the pain of believing my father would not have wanted me for his son.

Time heals … if you let it. Big if.

Who knew why Landis had taken his own life? He might have been gay; a third of all teen suicides are, but even if he hadn't been, that kind of humiliation would have been hard to get past. I tried to remember the adolescent mindset, the social hierarchy of high school life. Looking back from a safe distance, I think a shrewd eye and a sharp tongue had shielded me from my peers. *You're a sarcastic shit,* Rob used to say in compliment.

* * * * *

Bruce called as I was opening a can of dinner. I realized I hadn't finished listening to his earlier message.

"Where have you been all day? Why didn't you call?" he demanded first thing.

"I haven't had a chance." I filled him in briefly on what had been happening. Bruce listened impatiently and then said, "You shouldn't be alone."

"I'm okay." Here was one solution to spending a night alone with my memories and fears.

"I miss you."

"Bruce …"

"Let me come over."

"Not tonight." I tried to soften it. "I'm going to have an early night."

"You sound strange. What's wrong? We can have an early night together. Come on. Let me take care of you."

You need someone to take care of you, ma belle, Claude's ghost whispered. I felt that burn behind my eyes.

"Bruce," I said gently, "I need time to myself. I'm whipped."

"Why are you pushing me away?"

"I'm not. Bruce ..." I took a deep breath. "You're moving too fast for me."

There was a pause. "What does that mean?"

"It means, I need a little time."

"Space. You need space." I could hear the bitterness in his voice.

"What's wrong with that?"

"Why don't you just say what you mean?"

"I'm trying to."

"No. If I was the right person you wouldn't want time or space. You'd want to be with me like I want to be with you."

I didn't know if that was true or not. I said quietly, "Bruce, don't back me into a corner. It's just one night."

"That's what you think." He hung up.

I went through the video library seeking solace. Finally I settled on 1940's superb *The Sea Hawk* with Errol Flynn. They just don't build men like Errol anymore, I thought regretfully. I poured some brandy into my Ovaltine.

Not bad.

Next round I poured some Ovaltine into my brandy.

*　*　*　*　*

When I woke the lights were on, the TV was blaring commercials, and I had the echo of the phone in my ears. I lay there for a few moments blinking at the ceiling, wondering if I'd dreamed it.

The phone rang again.

I jumped off the couch and sprinted for the phone. I'm not sure who I was expecting. I picked the receiver up, croaked out something.

Dead air.

The hair on the back of my neck stood up. My heart skipped a beat.

"Hello?" I tried to sound flat and unimpressed. I should have stopped with one. The rest came out sounding like one of those woman-in-jeopardy extravaganzas on the Lifetime channel. *Hello? Hello? Hello?* when any rational person would have hung up and gone back to sleep.

I hung up.

The phone rang again.

I picked it up.

Heavy breathing. *"Adrien...."* A hoarse whisper that, despite common sense, turned my heart stammering and scared.

Up until then I guess I'd hoped the breather calls and frequent hang ups were random and unrelated.

"Adrien. I'm going to kill you."

The caller hung up.

I'm getting some weird calls, I'd told Jean at dinner. And Jean, always practical, responded, *Don't you have Caller ID? Did you try return dialing? Dial *69.*

I had Caller ID. I didn't recognize the number. I dialed *69. The phone rang and rang and then ... noise. Yelling ... cheerful yelling, like at a bar. Or was that a TV?

"Hello?" said Bruce doubtfully.

I hung up.

* * * * *

Two minutes after the emotional supernova, the phone rang again. My hand seemed to reach for it of its own accord.

Silence.

I managed to get the word out. "Bruce?"

"Adrien?" I knew his voice so well by now, and yet it was the voice of someone I didn't know at all.

I could sense him thinking it through, trying to read my mind. Wondering if I knew. Wondering how the hell I *couldn't.* Wondering why I didn't say something. I took a deep breath. "I-I hoped it was you. You're right. I don't want to be alone tonight."

There was bewilderment in the pause. Then, "What's happened?"

"Nothing. I just got this phone call a while ago. I ... need you." I didn't have to fake the choked voice. There was a rock in my throat.

This time he didn't hesitate. "I'm on my way."

I left a message at Hollywood Homicide. Then I dialed Riordan's home number. A woman's voice on the answering machine asked me to leave my important message at the beep. I sweated bullets then made my decision.

"It's Adrien English," I said. "My friend Bruce just called. Bruce Green, the reporter. I think he may have ... may be ...."

Even now it felt impossible to say what I believed. I already questioned my deductions. Bruce was jealous, possessive. Okay, maybe it was a bit adolescent, but who hasn't, at some point, driven past an ex-lover's house or been tempted to place an anonymous phone call? It wasn't wise, but was it necessarily sign of a deranged mind?

Was that all my suspicions were based on? I had no *proof* that these calls came from the same person sending flowers, stalking me. I had no proof my caller was my stalker. I had no proof my stalker had killed Robert and Claude. Hell, I had no proof that Robert and Claude's killer were the same.

The answering machine was recording my indecision. "I'm going over to his house." I didn't remember the house address, but I gave him the street and what the house looked like. "It's nine-thirty. If something happens to me ... ." I couldn't finish it. If I was wrong about Bruce this was an unforgivable betrayal. I had just offered his name up as a possible murder suspect to a homophobic cop — based on nothing more than his infatuation with me. I finished, "I'm going to try to get proof."

* * * * *

Bruce's house was dark but the porch light shone welcomingly as I walked up the sidewalk. I unlatched the side gate and walked around the back. Like I'd thought, a paved walkway with steps leading to a side entrance — nice to know my instincts were occasionally right. I skirted past the doorway and the requisite potted palms. Dry bougainvillea leaves crunched under foot, scuttled across the patio. The play-set in the jungle of weeds creaked, one swing swaying in the wind.

I took out my pocket knife and started prying at the screen fastenings of Bruce's bedroom window. I didn't know how long Bruce would wait at my place before he started back for home, but I was dogged by a frantic sense of hurry and danger.

I was lifting off the screen when a hand clamped down on my shoulder. I let out a muffled shriek before a second hand clamped over my mouth.

I swung blindly with the screen. It banged into the bushes and against the house.

"Knock it off!" hissed a voice against my ear as we grappled clumsily.

Recognizing the voice, I dropped the screen and quit struggling. Jerked my head free. "Are you trying to give me heart failure?" I gasped out.

"What the hell are you doing?" Detective Riordan's hands bit into my shoulders. "Why are you here?" His face in the moonlight was frightening and unfamiliar. When I realized what he thought I just stood there gaping.

"You don't think *I* —"

He yanked my sweater up and felt around my waist. Instinctively, I grabbed at his hands; he knocked them away. "Put 'em up." He wasn't kidding. One look at his face was all I needed. I locked my hands behind my head. Amazement held me silent as he roughly patted down my hips. One hand hooked in my belt, he nudged my legs apart with his own, and then knelt, running his hands down my legs. I stood there like an inner-city lawn ornament, as though I'd been getting frisked all my life.

Riordan stood up. "Are you crazy?"

"No, I —"

It was rhetorical because he bit out, "Hasn't your boyfriend given you a key yet?"

I took a couple of deep breaths. I was still shaky from the recent surge of adrenaline and fear. "It's not what you think. Whatever it is you're thinking now."

He said bleakly, "I'm thinking I've caught you breaking and entering twice. I'm thinking I told you not to go anywhere without notifying me first."

"I tried to call you. I left a message."

"For Christ's sake, are you … ." Words seemed to fail him.

"Listen to me." In my urgency I reached toward him. He looked down distractedly at my hand resting on his sleeve. "Something happened tonight. I think — I think Bruce —"

"No shit, Sherlock," he said grimly.

"I should have known," I said miserably. "The first guy I get involved with in years."

His laugh was nasty. "You sure can pick 'em. Do you know whose house this is?"

"Bruce's."

"This is where Grant Landis lived growing up. This is the house he supposedly died in."

I blinked up at him. "Supposedly?"

"Landis isn't dead. There's no death certificate."

"But … ." My voice died.

"His parents spread the word he was dead. He attempted suicide after graduating high school. He was institutionalized. After his release he disappeared."

"Why would his parents do that?"

He said acridly, "My take? They wished he *was* dead. I think he was kept locked up as much for being queer as for trying to off himself."

My throat hurt. I said, "But Bruce —"

"Bruce *is* Landis. Until six years ago Bruce Green didn't exist. No DMV records, no TRW report — there's no trace of him before that." His hand closed on my arm, steering me toward the gate. "We don't have time to chat. I don't know where he went but he's liable to be back any minute."

"He went to see me."

"Huh?"

"I called him. Asked him to come over so I could —"

"So you could *what?* Jesus H. Christ! Don't you get it? This guy kills people!"

"Yes, I get it! You said you had to have proof. *I* had to have proof before I could — turn him over."

That grip on my arm was going to leave bruises. "I asked you to stay out of it. I specifically told you. What do I have to do? Arrest you?"

"Anything to get me in handcuffs?"

I don't know why that popped out, but police brutality seemed imminent.

I rushed on, "You're a cop. You said yourself, your hands are tied."

"Look ma, no hands." Riordan showed me his empty hands. "Fine. You wanted to help. You helped. Now get your ass out of here."

"You're not listening. I may be able to —" Finish a sentence? Not likely with Detective Riordan. Once again he cut over me.

"No, *you're* not listening. This is a police investigation. I'm already hanging in the wind conducting an unauthorized surveillance." He gave me a slight shove. "Vamoose."

I shoved back. "Stop pushing me."

For a minute I thought we were going to get into a wrestling match. The tension wasn't all due to the uncertainty and threat.

"This is my life. I have a say in what happens to me."

"What does that mean?"

I had no idea, but I was tired of being on the receiving end. I ignored him, started walking back to the gate.

Riordan called suddenly, "Damn. Adrien, wait. Wait. Change of plan. I want you to go swear out a complaint against Green. Will you do that?"

I stopped walking. "What? Why?"

His expression was unreadable in the moonlight. "Chan's trying to get a search warrant, but if you swear out a complaint we can pick Green up immediately on the stalker charge."

"You think a restraining order is going to stop him?"

"Trust me, would you?"

He was kind of asking a lot, seeing my life was at stake. When I didn't instantly react he ran both hands over his pale hair and exclaimed, "Adrien, would you GO?"

Until then I hadn't realized how on edge he was. Now I could feel it, like an electrical field around him.

"I'm going."

* * * * *

I vamoosed back to where I'd parked the Bronco a couple of blocks down.

I was crossing the street when an approaching car caught me in its headlights. It slowed. Stopped. The window rolled down.

"Adrien?"

I froze.

"What are you doing here? I went to your place."

Say something, I urged myself. Say something before he stomps on the accelerator and mows you down. "I'm sorry!" I called. "I was too jumpy to wait. I'm ... uh ... I'm afraid I'm being watched."

"By the police?"

"No. Yes. I don't know." Brilliant. Grace Latham herself couldn't have done better.

"What did you park down here for?" The frown was in his voice.

"I'm not thinking clearly," I said honestly. "I'm afraid."

"Of what?"

Of you. I wasn't sure I could make it across the street, unlock the Bronco and get in before he overtook me. I could start yelling for Riordan, but I doubted if he'd hear me this far down the block. Proof. We needed proof.

I shivered and said, "Are we going to stand out here talking all night?"

I saw him reach across and unlock the door. "Get in."

I got in.

In silence we drove up the street to the yellow and brown house. The garage door opened and we slipped under into the close darkness. The garage door rumbled shut.

Bruce turned off the car engine.

I've never been claustrophobic but I felt an overwhelming sense of danger pressing in on me as I sat next to Bruce in the dead of night.

Finally he moved and said, "Well? Coming?"

CHAPTER FIFTEEN

"**Y**ou're so tense tonight." Bruce leaned over on his elbow and kissed the nape of my neck.

I lay naked on my stomach beside him, feeling vulnerable with my back exposed; but the less he read of my face the better. The screen was still off the bedroom window. Bruce hadn't noticed in the darkness, but I had. I kept reassuring myself that Riordan was out there — somewhere. Nothing would happen to me if I kept my head.

Then I started worrying about what might happen if the police suddenly burst in on us. How might Bruce react? I didn't want to be caught in the crossfire.

"I'm not feeling too hot," I excused myself to Bruce. "My heart's bothering me a little."

"Yeah?"

Not completely a lie. I felt sick with nerves and dread. But my heart was holding steady despite its desire to climb into my mouth and hide.

What if Riordan had gone haring back to my place before Bruce and I drove up? What if he had no idea where I was? What if right this minute he was busy getting paperwork together so I could swear out a complaint against Bruce?

Bruce slid a hand down my spine and I gave a shudder. He chuckled.

"Cold?" He rubbed his foot up and down my calf.

I listened tautly to what sounded like a floor board creaking. Rolled onto my side and wound my arms around Bruce's shoulders. He kissed me hungrily, his mouth wet and hot. I made some small sound. Mostly dismay.

Bruce whispered, "Hell, your heart *is* beating fast." He let go of me, rolled over and off the bed. "I'll get your pills."

"*No —*" I dived, grabbing his arm before he could walk back into the living room where we'd shucked our clothes fifteen minutes earlier. Bruce gazed down at me, his face unreadable in the light from the hall.

"It's okay," I babbled. "I'm not sick. Just wound up. Hand me the wine."

I reached for the pink goblet on the bedstand and nearly knocked over the clock. The luminous numbers flipped over like game show cards ticking off the last minutes of my life.

Bruce sat down beside me once more, stroking me while I sipped.

"I love you, Adrien."

I lowered my lashes. Not even to save my life, I thought. To lie about that seemed worse than anything anyone had done to him yet.

"Tonight I thought...."

I put the glass down, leaned back into the pillows. I reached out to him.

"I thought you didn't want me," he muttered. He sounded close to tears. I felt like crying myself. I stroked his back.

"I couldn't bear that, Adrien."

"Don't."

"It's been different with you from the beginning. From the first time I ever saw you. I didn't think I could still feel this way, but I do. I do."

"You don't have to tell me."

He put his hand between my thighs, cupping my balls. I caught my breath.

His lopsided smile was intimate. "Is this good?"

"You know it is."

He nodded, fingering me knowledgeably. "I know you."

The incredible thing was that knowing what I knew, scared to death as I was, and even conscious that Riordan might be somewhere nearby, my body did respond. I did feel something for him, beyond the horror and fear. I couldn't forget the teenage boy who had wanted to die. I couldn't forget what had happened to him, the pain and fear and isolation that turned him into a monster. A monster whose tears wet my fingertips.

He got on his knees in a quick move. Leaned forward, his breath hot against my face. "Tell me what you want, Adrien." He was poised over me. Massive. A mountain. A landslide ready to fall and bury me alive. "Say it. You know you want it."

I rested my hand against his face, feeling the bristle on his jaw. He turned his head. Bit my fingers.

"You want me to fuck you?"

Guilt? Grief? Reciprocity?

"Yes," I said huskily.

He guided me back onto my belly. His hands were shaking and he wasn't the only one. I rested my face on my folded arms, heart thudding. His hands slid over my ass, caressing roughly, spreading my cheeks. Two wet fingers slid in without ceremony. I bit my lip, trying to relax rigid muscles. I wasn't a virgin, but it had been a very long time for me.

Bruce mumbled inarticulate words of apology and love.

"It's all right," I said.

He pushed in and I had to bite my arm to keep from crying out. It wasn't just the lack of preparation; he wasn't wearing a condom. Jesus. I remembered telling Riordan I was strictly a safe sex guy, and now here I was engaging in unprotected sex with a homicidal maniac. Define safe, Adrien.

I closed my eyes, tried to regulate my breathing while Bruce humped against my ass. Awkward and anguished, his fingers clawed into my hips, trying to position me, thrusting wildly, frantically; an angry blind man flailing out with his cane.

I agreed to this, I thought dizzily. I let myself in for it. *Shut up and deal with it because if you yell, someone is going to die. Probably you.*

My breath huffed out in pained pants as Bruce rocked harder, faster. He reached beneath my belly and gave my cock a yank. It hurt.

I smothered my groan in my arm. Fought the pricking behind my eyes.

"I love you. I love you," he panted. "You're mine. You know that. Mine. Forever."

He began to come, collapsing on top of me in a shuddering sweaty heap. His silent tears trickled down my back.

Once Bruce fell asleep it was eerily quiet. I was afraid to move.

I lay still, ears attuned, waiting.

A soft sound from down the hallway.

I lifted my head. Hesitated. Bruce slumbered on, sleeping the peaceful sleep of the conscienceless. Cautiously I inched away, eased off the bed. The springs protested. I stopped. No movement from Bruce. I tiptoed to the door.

We'd left the lights on when we had retired, and I had a clear view of Riordan standing at the far end of the hall. He had his gun out. It looked like a cannon. He stared at me for a long moment. Then he gestured soundlessly, beckoning me toward him: *Get out now.*

Bruce sat up in the bed behind me. I froze.

"What are you doing?" He sounded fully awake.

"Nothing." I hesitated. Everything in me said "run." But the realization of what was about to happen...it's difficult to explain how terrifying I found that vision of impending violence. I don't know if I thought I could avert it, but I was compelled to try and postpone it.

"What are you looking for? Come back to bed."

I said huskily, "It's late. I should go."

"Come back to bed, Adrien." There was something in his voice. A short while ago I had lain in his arms. I could still taste him. I came back to bed. Sat down as gingerly as though on broken glass.

He said tenderly, indulgently, "What's wrong?"

"Nothing." Even I could hear the strain in my voice.

Silence.

Then he said flatly, "Oh."

One scant syllable, but I knew. I knew and he knew. All evening we had pretended. Postponed what we both knew in our hearts.

In one fast, lithe movement, Bruce was off the bed. He walked over to the bedroom door and slammed it, shutting us into total darkness. I could hear my quick breaths and the scratch of the twigs at the window. There was just enough light from the waning moon to see his silhouette unmoving where he stood by the door.

I sat there wordlessly, reassuring myself that he couldn't have seen Riordan hovering down the hall. Riordan would have ducked back, right?

"Bruce," I began.

"I know, Adrien." He spoke consolingly, as though he understood why I had done what I had. His silhouette moved over to the dresser and vanished into the deeper shadows. I heard the slide of the drawers. The soft rustle of clothes. It was more terrifying not to be able to see him. Then I caught his reflection in the mirror, the pale glimmer of his body. He turned, and in the gloom I could just discern the outline of white — a grim smile that wasn't Bruce. Wasn't human in fact. A mask. A skull mask which he was unhurriedly adjusting over his head.

I backed off the bed, knocked into the bedstand and reached automatically to save the lamp. Bruce felt around in the drawer, the mask still staring my way. Hypnotized I watched him raise something up, saw the glint of light on silver. A blade.

"What are you doing?" I was surprised to hear my voice at all, let alone sounding almost level.

"What does it look like I'm doing?" He walked toward me, knife upheld. It was stagy. Unreal.

I reached over and turned on the lamp beside the bed.

Like a true creature of the night, he paused. There's something about light. Even the 60 watt household variety.

"Turn that out," he said hoarsely.

I shook my head. I couldn't tear my eyes away from the knife. It looked huge. Sharp. A butcher's knife. I pictured it sliding into my chest. With an effort I kicked my brain into gear.

"Bruce, why are you doing this?"

"Now *that's* a silly question."

"Bruce —"

"Don't call me that."

"What do you want me to call you? Grant?"

He stood motionless as though testing the power of his name on himself.

"Take the mask off," I said. "Since we're not pretending."

"I like it. You know why? Because it's symbolic. You know? Everyone wears masks. Everyone puts on a face of what they want you to see. Even death."

Murdered *and* lectured in one night. It really was too much.

He laughed muffledly. "And the main thing is, it scares you. I like that. You should see your face. I'm surprised you haven't keeled over yet. That would be ironic, wouldn't it?"

"I don't think ironic is the right word." I wondered what Riordan was doing. What was he waiting for? In five minutes I could be dead. In three minutes. In fact, it wouldn't take Bruce more than a minute to take care of me. I tried to imagine wrestling him for the knife and knew talking was my best bet.

"What is the right word?" Bruce inquired. "Betrayed? *Fucked?*"

I swallowed hard.

"What? No famous last words?" Bruce advanced. "Truth hurts, doesn't it?" He gave that unnerving rubbery laugh. "So does this, by the way."

I licked my lips. "Don't I get to hear why?"

"Why what?"

"Why you killed Rob and the others. Andy ... ." Suddenly I couldn't remember their names.

"I didn't kill Andy." He sounded offended. "God killed Andy. That was the sign I was on the right path."

"You think God wants you to kill people because of a high school prank?"

"*Prank?* That prank destroyed my life. Ruined me. You have no idea what you're talking about!"

"So explain it to me."

His eyes studied me through the eye holes in the mask. "Believe me, you won't agree with my reasoning. I've tried explaining before. How's this? Everything that has happened to me happened because of Robert Hersey and his sycophantic buddies. Everything."

"That's not reasonable, Br — Grant. You're too smart to believe —"

He interrupted casually, "But enough about me. This is about you."

"Me?"

"Yes, you. YOU, YOU, YOU!" He started jabbing at the air, yelling it.

Something horrifyingly like a sob tore out of my throat.

Bruce stopped. "Don't cry," he said kindly. "Everything dies eventually." He pointed the knife at me, like a professor with a pointer.

"Anyway, it's your own fault, isn't it? I want you to know that I would never have hurt you. Never. You made this happen. Not me. I always liked you, even though you *never* noticed me." His hand slashed through the air. "NEVER NOTICED —"

I flinched as the knife carved a long rip through the flowered wallpaper. I tried to think what to do if he came across the bed. I'd be cornered. I was cornered now. I'd be cornered in a tighter space. Less time to die in.

He calmed again. "I tried to get all my classes with you. I used to always sit behind you. Remember? Pathetic, isn't it? You even came to this house once, you know. I couldn't believe you didn't remember."

I got control of my voice. "Did you want me to remember?"

He seemed to consider this. "When I saw you in the church I wanted to protect you from those fucking cops. But the truth is, you like those fucking cops, don't you? You like that blond one."

"Speaking of cops," I got out. "Bruce, you have to know you aren't going to get away with this. They will lock you up forever."

"I don't want to get away with it. Not anymore." He added, "And no, they won't."

Keep him talking. Riordan had to be on the other side of that door. If I could just get to it before Bruce stabbed me. "If I can figure it out, the cops can."

"Don't bet on it."

I edged toward the door. "Tell me something. Why Claude? What did he ever do to you?"

"Who? Oh, the black dude. Well, that was your fault too, Adrien. You canceled our evening together, didn't you? You wouldn't explain why, you just blew me off. So I followed you to see where you were going. I was parked down the street the whole time we were talking. I was on my cell phone." He sounded innocently pleased with his own cleverness. "Call forwarding."

"You were spying on me?" Don't ask, but my life probably forfeit, I still felt a flare of indignation.

He answered defensively, "I couldn't wait to see you again. I used to park there under the trees and watch that asshole Robert. And then I started watching you. I followed you that evening to see what you were up to, and once I knew, I took care of that black bastard." He shrugged. "I thought that would get your attention."

My nerve gave out and I ran for the door. Bruce got there first and blocked it squarely. He raised the knife. His laugh was coming out weirdly behind the plastic face. He adjusted his grip on the knife handle, the better for slicing me to ribbons. I took a step back.

"I wondered what this would feel like when it happened," he said slowly.

"Me too." I couldn't take my eyes off the knife.

"I think it could have worked for us."

My heart was pounding so hard in my throat it was hard to get the words out. "It would have been hard with you murdering my friends every time you needed my attention."

Bruce reached up with the knife to scratch his forehead. The point punctured the mask and a tiny drop of blood showed. As I stared, it welled and then trickled slowly down the skull face.

"I do love you," whispered Bruce. "There's nothing left for me without you." There were tears in his voice.

"Bruce," I pleaded, "Think it through." *Riordan, where the fuck are you?*

"We'll die together like true lovers should. Like Romeo and ... ." unnervingly he giggled. "Romeo."

Blabbing the first thing that came to me, I said desperately, "Sure, but *then* what happens?"

"What?"

There was movement outside the window. We both looked around and then Bruce grabbed me with his free arm, dragging me in front of him as an iron lawn chair came crashing through the bedroom window, followed by Riordan.

It was like in the movies. He hit the floor in a shoulder roll and came up on one knee with his gun aimed at us. The detached part of my brain that was still taking notes admired the smooth efficiency of that.

Bruce kept me pinned close, arm about my throat, using me as a shield. His breath was hot in my ear, his cheek resting against mine. I could feel his sweat against my skin — or maybe it was my own sweat. I could also feel that he had a hard-on, and that was the most unnerving thing of all.

I was pretty sure that I was really going to die in the next minute or two. I'd thought a lot about death over the years, but I never pictured checking out like this.

"Put down the knife." Riordan sounded calm and instructive.

Bruce on the other hand was shaking with excitement. The hand holding the knife to my throat was so rigid it had a tremor.

"No! Put down the gun. I'll kill him if you don't!"

I heard myself say, "He'll kill me anyway."

A bar seemed to clamp down, closing off my windpipe. "Shut up!" Bruce said from underwater. Stars shot through the darkness flooding up around me. I wheezed, let myself go heavy.

Bruce's arm eased up. I gulped oxygen. Heard Riordan soothing, "No he won't. That wouldn't be smart. Bruce is too smart for that, right Bruce?"

"Shut up," Bruce said again.

I gulped oxygen. Regained my footing.

Riordan was still trying to reassure us all that it was under control. "Bruce doesn't want to hurt you, do you, Bruce? Let's talk for a minute. Let's talk about —"

"Let's talk about this!" Bruce made a sudden gesture. There was a bright pain beneath my ear.

At the same instant Riordan yelled, "*Bruce* — I'll blow your fucking head off!" He was standing just a few feet from us. The gun aimed at my head seemed huge. I could look right down the barrel. It was like a tunnel.

Riordan said, "I'll splatter your brains all over that goddamn wall." He sounded a little breathless.

"I don't care," sobbed Bruce. He could cry and still hold the knife in place. The pain at my jaw seemed to pause. I could feel something hot trickling down my neck. Jesus, had he cut my throat?

"Yes, you do. You want all the world to know how smart you are. You want Adrien to know how smart you are."

"Wrong again. WRONG! You don't know shit!"

"I know that I've radioed for help. I know that in minutes this place will be swarming with cops. Listen."

We listened. The wail of sirens had been growing steadily louder, but I don't think I'd heard it until then. Now it was earsplitting.

Bruce's hold shifted. "It doesn't matter." He said, and all at once he sounded calm. Serene. Not a good sign, I recognized instinctively.

I met Riordan's eyes. Up until now he had not looked directly at me. I didn't know if I was reading him right or not, but I dug my fingers into the pressure point of Bruce's forearm. At the same time I hooked my right foot around his and yanked him off balance. Textbook Tai Chi. I couldn't believe it when it worked.

There was an incredible explosion that seemed to ricochet off the walls. Plaster peppered the side of my face and hair. The arm holding me fell away. The blade at my throat dropped, scratched a crescent across my chest and ribs, tore the fleshy part of my forearm as it sliced downward.

I stumbled away in a kind of daze.

Riordan fired again looking like a poster boy for the NRA. Perfect stance. Perfect aim. As I stared a great red bloom seemed to blossom in the center of Bruce's chest. The crimson spread. In slow motion he slid down the wall. Languidly he sprawled onto the carpet. Red-black smeared the wall behind him. The bedroom door opened, swinging silently wide.

Bruce's fingers slowly released the knife, uncurling gently. The eyes behind the mask were closed.

The dead don't close their eyes. As this thought ran through my brain, Bruce's eyes opened. They gazed at the carpet with a fixed look that living eyes never have.

"Okay, baby?"

Riordan was walking toward me. I realized he was talking to me.

I rummaged around inside my head. Found words. "Yeah." My voice cracked and I had to try again. "Thanks. Thank you."

His hand slid across my bare shoulder, fastened around the back of my neck, drew me forward. I reeled against him, my head resting for a moment in the curve of his neck and shoulder, tried to catch my breath. His heart was thudding a million miles an hour. His chest rising and falling. Neither of us said a word.

The sirens sounded like they were in the kitchen. The banging on the front door seemed to shake the whole house. Riordan holstered his gun, pulled his ID, and stepped in front of me as the front door gave with a crash and a dozen uniforms burst into the living room with weapons drawn.

* * * * *

"It was a righteous shooting," Chan said for the third time.

It was close to dawn. I was dressed. My chest was taped and my arm and throat bandaged by the paramedics. I had answered a million questions, and now I stood with Chan outside the house while the crime scene team bustled about their grisly business.

Black-and-whites were angled all over the street. The Landis yard and sidewalk had been sectioned off. Even at this hour of the morning a crowd was forming behind the yellow crime scene tape. Overhead, birds were starting to twitter in the trees.

"I've been writing a book myself," Chan said confidentially, taking a long drag on his cigarette. "I was wondering if you might be willing to read it sometime. You know, give me your honest opinion."

"Sure." Vainly, I searched the swarm of uniforms and plainclothes for Riordan.

"It's a police procedural."

I nodded, not listening.

Riordan materialized before us. He said to Chan, "I think I'll drive Mr. English home, Paul."

Chan had a funny look on his face. "Uh ...what about IA?"

"What about 'em?"

Chan glanced at me and shrugged. Flicked the cigarette onto the porch and ground it out with his heel.

We slipped under the crime scene tape. Made our way through the crowd that parted warily before us. In silence, we walked down the shady street to where I'd left the Bronco — a lifetime ago.

Riordan reached his palm out. I handed my keys over. He unlocked my door. Walked around, unlocked the driver's side, and climbed in beside me.

He started the engine.

I said, "I don't know your first name."

"Jake." He looked at me briefly. Looked away.

More silence while the engine warmed. Riordan yawned hugely, scrubbed his face with his hands. His glance slid my way. "You know, this won't be an easy thing, Adrien."

An officer-involved shooting was not going to be fun, righteous or not.

"The investigation you mean?"

"No." He gave me that crooked smile. "No, I don't mean that."

I stared out at the first blush of sunrise lighting the surrounding Chatsworth hills.

Despite myself, I started to smile.

AUTHOR'S NOTE

As of this revision, *Fatal Shadows* is sixteen years old. A lot of things have changed since I first wrote the story of Adrien English, and I mean besides Robinsons-May no longer existing. Were I to write this story today, it would be a vastly different story. But to rewrite it now would be to try and erase the past, and that's always dangerous.

ALSO BY JOSH LANYON

NOVELS

The ADRIEN ENGLISH Mysteries

Fatal Shadows

A Dangerous Thing

The Hell You Say

Death of a Pirate King

The Dark Tide

Stranger Things Have Happened

The HOLMES & MORIARITY Mysteries

Somebody Killed His Editor

All She Wrote

The Boy With the Painful Tattoo

A SHOT IN THE DARK Series

This Rough Magic

The ALL'S FAIR Series

Fair Game

Fair Play

OTHER NOVELS

The Ghost Wore Yellow Socks

Mexican Heat (with Laura Baumbach)

Strange Fortune

Come Unto These Yellow Sands

Stranger on the Shore

NOVELLAS

The DANGEROUS GROUND Series

Dangerous Ground

Old Poison

Blood Heat

Dead Run

kick Start

The I SPY Series

I Spy Something Bloody

I Spy Something Wicked

I Spy Something Christmas

The IN A DARK WOOD Series

In a Dark Wood

The Parting Glass

The DARK HORSE Series

The Dark Horse

The White Knight

The DOYLE & SPAIN Series

Snowball in Hell

The HAUNTED HEART Series

Haunted Heart: Winter

The XOXO FILES Series

Mummy Dearest (XOXO FILES Series)

OTHER NOVELLAS

Cards on the Table

The Dark Farewell

The Darkling Thrush

The Dickens with Love

Don't Look Back

A Ghost of a Chance

Lovers and Other Strangers

Out of the Blue

A Vintage Affair

Lone Star (in Men Under the Mistletoe)

Green Glass Beads (in Irregulars)

Blood Red Butterfly

Everything I Know

SHORT STORIES

A Limited Engagement

The French Have a Word for It

In Sunshine or In Shadow

Until We Meet Once More

Icecapade (in His for the Holidays)

Perfect Day

Heart Trouble

In Plain Sight

Merry Christmas, Darling (Holiday Codas)

The PETIT MORTS Stories (*SWEET SPOT* Collection)

Other People's Weddings

Slings and Arrows

Sort of Stranger Than Fiction

Critic's Choice

Just Desserts

COLLECTIONS

The Adrien English Mysteries

Collected Novellas, Vol. 1

Collected Novellas, Vol. 2

Armed & Dangerous

In From the Cold: The I Spy Stories

In Sunshine or In Shadow

Sweet Spot

Male/Male Mystery & Suspense Box Set

NON-FICTION

Man, Oh Man!: Writing Quality M/M Fiction

ABOUT THE AUTHOR

A distinct voice in gay fiction, multi-award-winning author JOSH LANYON has been writing gay mystery, adventure and romance for over a decade. In addition to numerous short stories, novellas, and novels, Josh is the author of the critically acclaimed Adrien English series, including *The Hell You Say*, winner of the 2006 USABookNews awards for GLBT Fiction. Josh is an Eppie Award winner and a three-time Lambda Literary Award finalist.

For more information, go to **www.joshlanyon.com**, or follow Josh on **Twitter**, **Facebook**, and **Goodreads**.

AN EXCERPT FROM

A
DANGEROUS
THING

THE ADRIEN ENGLISH MYSTERIES
BOOK TWO

JOSH LANYON

CHAPTER ONE

She was young and she was lovely and she was dead. Very dead.

And this was bad. Very bad.

What had once been Lavinia was now an ungraceful sprawl of long blonde hair and long white limbs — and then Jason's horrified brain recognized what his eyes had refused to see: Lavinia's slender arms ended in two bloody stumps.

I stopped typing, read it back and winced. Poor Jason. We had been stuck discovering Lavinia's body for the past two days and we still couldn't get it right.

I hit the delete key.

Lousy as was *Titus Andronicus*, my second Jason Leland mystery, *Death for a Deadly Deed*, was even worse. I guess basing Jason's second outing on Shakespeare's infamous play was only the first of my mistakes. I was still brooding when the phone rang.

"It's me," Jake said. "I can't make it tonight."

"It's okay," I said. "I wasn't expecting you."

Silence.

I let it stretch, which is not like me, being the civilized guy I am.

"Adrien?" Jake asked at last.

"Yo?"

"I'm a cop. It's who I am. It's what I do."

"You sound like the lead-in to a TV show." Before he could hit back, I added, "Don't sweat it, Jake. I'll find something else to do tonight."

Silence.

I realized I'd deleted too much from my manuscript. Was I supposed to hit Edit and then Undo? Or just Undo? Or Control + Z? Word Perfect I am not.

"Have fun," Jake said pleasantly, and rang off.

"See ya," I muttered to the dial tone.

These dreary dumps I call my life, as the bard would say.

For a moment I sat there staring at the blinking cursor on my screen. It occurred to me that I needed to make some changes — and not just in *Death for a Deadly Deed*.

Swearing under my breath, I hit Save and closed the document. Exit and Shut Down. See how easy that was?

I went downstairs to the shop where Angus, my assistant (and resident warlock), was slicing open a shipment of books with a utility knife.

"Hey, I'm going out of town," I announced as Angus gazed entranced at a best-selling cover featuring a blood-spattered ax.

I wasn't sure if I had a dial tone or not. He didn't blink. Angus is tall, raw-boned, and pale as a ghost. Jake has a number of unkind sobriquets for him, but the kid is smart and hardworking. I figure that's all that is my business.

"Why?" he mumbled at last.

"Because I need a vacation. Because I can't write with all these distractions."

At last Angus tore his bespectacled gaze from the gory dust jacket. "Why?"

After a couple of months I was becoming fluent in Anguspeak.

"The way it is, man. Can you keep an eye on things?" Keep the Black Masses to a minimum and not eat all fifty boxes of gourmet cookies in the storeroom?

Angus shrugged. "I guess. Class starts back up in two weeks though."

I've never been able to ascertain exactly what Angus is studying at UCLA. Library Science or Demonology 101?

"I'll be back by then. I just want to get away for a few days."

"Where are you going?" This was the most interest in my actions Angus had shown in two months.

"I own property up north in Sonora. Accurately, outside of Sonora near a little town called Basking. I thought I'd drive up there." I added, "Tonight."

"Tonight?"

"It's four-thirty now. It shouldn't take me more than six or seven hours."

Angus mulled this over, absently testing the point of the utility knife with his thumb.

"It's not like you to be impulsive, Adrien," was his verdict. "What do I tell that cop of yours?"

"He's not my actual personal property," I said shortly. "He's a public servant." In more ways than one. "Anyway you won't have to tell him anything because I don't plan on seeing him anytime soon."

"Oh." Angus looked down at the knife with a small smile. Tiffs among the faggots were apparently the stuff of quiet merriment.

I left Angus with visions of dismemberment still dancing in his head and went to pack. It didn't take long to throw a couple of pairs of Levi's and a toothbrush into my Gladstone. I emptied the fridge into an ice chest, dug out my sleeping bag and tossed computer disks and a couple of CDs in with my clothes and laptop.

By a quarter after six I was fighting the workday traffic as I headed the Bronco out toward Magic Mountain and the 5 Freeway. Over the pass it was bumper to bumper, but what the hell, I had a thermos full of Gevalia Popayan coffee, Patty Griffin's *Flaming Red* rocking on the CD player, and I was heading in the right direction — away from Jake.

* * * * *

Outside Mojave I pulled in for gas at a quaint filling station surrounded by Joshua trees and stacks of old tires. An enormous purple gorilla balloon floated overhead as an advertising gimmick. I pumped gas and enjoyed an *Apocalypse Now* sunset while the giant balloon bobbed gently on the desert breeze. For some reason the grape ape reminded me of Jake.

Jake. If only it were as easy to leave behind my preoccupation with Jake as it was to leave the city lights now twinkling in my rearview mirror.

Two months earlier Detective Jake Riordan had saved my life in what the papers unimaginatively called the "Gay Slasher Killings." When it was all over, Jake had received an official reprimand from the LAPD brass — and I had received an overture of sorts from Jake, a homosexual cop buried so deep in the closet *he* didn't know where to look for himself.

Riordan was tough and smart and handsome; and, other than that self-loathing hang-up, pretty much all I could have asked for in a potential mate. But gradually little things — like the fact he couldn't bear to touch me — began to take their toll. Okay, I exaggerate. He did put an arm around my shoulders once when we were watching a PBS documentary on hate crimes against gays. And he had taken to hugging me goodbye. It wasn't that Riordan was a virgin. Far from it. He was heavily into the S/M scene. But when it came to face-to-face, eye-to-eye, mouth-to-mouth, the Master turned into a schoolboy.

Witness our first and only necking session.

Riordan's mouth was a kiss away from my own when he gave a strange laugh and pulled back.

"Shit. I can't do this." He ran a hand through his blond hair, looked at me sideways.

"Can't do what? Kiss me?"

He shook his head and then nodded.

"My mouthwash isn't working? What's the problem?"

Jake made a sound that was supposed to pass for a laugh. He didn't answer.

"Why, Jake?" I asked quietly.

He blurted, "I open my eyes and I see the pores of your skin — your skin's okay, don't take this wrong — but you've got five o'clock shadow. You smell like aftershave. Your lips —" He gestured briefly and hopelessly. "It's just — you're not a chick."

"You noticed." I sounded flippant but I was thinking hard. "So this is a new experience for you? You have sex with guys but you don't —"

"It's nothing like this," Jake interrupted. "This is like *dating*. This is... weird."

Yeah, and whips, chains, scourges and blindfolds were normal?

"I could let you tie me up and beat the shit out of me, but will you still respect me in the morning?"

"I don't want you that way," he said. "I know you. It wouldn't be the same."

Swell. He preferred humiliating strange men in costume to kissing a man he knew. And presumably liked.

"Let me get this straight. You don't want to have sex with me?"

"Obviously I want to have sex with you."

Obviously. What was *I* thinking?

"But?"

He said impatiently, "I don't know! Why don't we watch a video or something?"

We watched a lot of videos. I was now an expert on the films of Steven Seagal and Vin Diesel, and I'd seen more Super Hero movies in the past month than I'd seen my entire childhood. It wasn't all *cinéma vérité*. We even went out for a couple of tense dinners. I guessed that Riordan was wary some of his copper pals might spot him fraternizing with a known homo, although he was too gentlemanly to say so aloud.

Mostly we talked. At my place. Behind closed doors. Not exactly heart to heart, but Jake talked about his work and his family: Mom, Dad, two brothers (one in the Police Academy), all under the delusion that James Patrick Riordan was as straight as the proverbial arrow.

Or mostly Jake talked. My role was usually listener. Occasionally he'd asked me questions which I labeled under the general heading of Gay Lifestyle: How many times a month did I have sex? (Uh … were we going by Terrestrial Dynamical Time?) When had I come out? (After college — when it was too late for mother to ground me.) Where did I go to meet guys? (Crime scenes?)

Even though Jake was older and probably more experienced, I sometimes felt like his gay mentor or Fag Big Brother. What I didn't feel like was his lover.

A month of tentative keeping company and then a month of excuses and canceled engagements.

It was over before it began.

"Look," I told him one night when he arrived four hours late for another dinner under wraps, "You're just going through the motions. Why bother?"

That tawny gaze lit on mine. Jake said bluntly, "I never meant to get involved with you, Adrien."

"Rest easy; you're not."

"Yeah, I am." And he put his big paw over mine.

Pathetic, but this is the kind of thing that kept me holding on. I use the term "holding on" loosely, because for the most part life went on exactly as before, with the exception of the funny flutter my heart gave when I'd hear Riordan's voice on the other end of the phone — and for all I knew that was incipient heart failure.

It sure as hell wasn't love, because I refused to do something so self-destructive as love a man who hated himself for being homosexual — which, by extension, probably meant he subconsciously hated me too. I reassured myself that although I liked Riordan, I wasn't closing any doors, wasn't missing out on any opportunities; I was still open to meeting new people, making new friends and lovers.

So why the frustration and anger, sure, even hurt, when the big guy pulled the plug as he had this evening?

* * * * *

Outside Bakersfield I made a pit stop at a rest area. I walked around and stretched my legs, bought a stale blueberry bagel from a catering truck and rechecked my *Thomas Guide* in the cab light of the SUV.

The full moon shone brightly, illuminating rolling hills dotted with oaks and occasional farmhouse lights. Miles of nothing but empty highway and starry skies. Miles of nothing but more miles as I headed north with the big rigs. I was doing about eighty-five, kicked back on cruise control with nothing to do but think and remember.

It was twenty-four years since I had last seen Pine Shadow Ranch. That was the summer before my Grandmother Anna died. I was eight years old, and summer vacations with Granna were the happiest times of my life.

Granna was kind of a family legend. One of those Roaring Twenties gals, she'd ditched her society husband and returned to her birthplace to raise horses and hell, as the mood took her. I remembered her as a rail-thin, tall woman with a silver bob and deeply tanned skin. My granny rolled her own cigarettes, rode like a bronc-buster and cussed in Italian — which was the language of her childhood nanny. It must have been some childhood judging from the frequency and fluency of her swearing.

There had been no hint that particular summer was to be the last. But two weeks after I returned to my mother's fretting bosom, my grandmother had been killed in a fall from a horse. To my mother's chagrin Granna bequeathed her entire estate to me. True, Granna's estate was nothing to rival the fortune left in trust to Lisa by my dear departed dad, but it was enough to ensure financial necessity would never tie me to Ma's apron strings.

I inherited half that money when I turned twenty-one, and I had spent it purchasing what was now Cloak and Dagger Books. I would inherit the balance when I turned forty, which around tax time seemed like a lifetime away. As for Pine Shadow Ranch, I'd had some furniture shipped down to me but had never gone back, preferring to remember it as it had been. There was a caretaker who kept an eye on the holdings, but for all I knew the place could have fallen to rack and ruin by the time I decided to take my 400-mile drive down memory lane.

* * * * *

It was nearly eleven when State Highway 49 narrowed to pine trees and mountains. I cracked the window. The night air was startlingly cold and clean with the bite of distant snow.

The next eighty miles of winding road were spent sandwiched between one of those monster trucks (high beams trained on my rearview) and a battered pickup with the license plate URUGLY. At five-mile intervals we would come to another blind curve and the monster truck would swing out in the opposite lane in a playful gambit of vehicular Russian roulette. And thirty seconds later he would drop back into formation just in time to avoid plowing into an oncoming car.

At last he made his big play, risked his all, and roared off around a bend, just missing a head-on with a logging truck. He vanished into the diesel-scented night.

Now it was just me and the forty-five-mile-an-hour wit in the pickup. Emptying the last of the Popayan coffee into my thermos cup, I fiddled with the radio trying to find a station that varied the thematic content of tears-in-the-beer, crying-on-the-shoulder-of-the-road, and hanging-onto-nothing-but-the-wheel. Despite the caffeine overload I was beat and my eyes felt ready to drop out of my head.

Fast approaching the stage of exhaustion where I wasn't sure if I was still driving or if I was only dreaming I was still driving, I nearly missed the turn off. The next ten miles were a challenge to the Bronco's shocks as well as my own, but at last I recognized the landmark of Saddleback Mountain and knew the Pine Shadow Ranch lay right around the next bend.

I downshifted as we began our descent. The Bronco rattled across a cattle guard. Ahead, the ranch lay motionless in the bright moonlight; from a distance it seemed untouched by time. Despite the dark windows and empty corrals I could almost convince myself that I was coming home, that someone waited to welcome me.

Drawing closer, I discerned the sign mounted on wooden posts above the open gate. Wood-burned letters had once spelled out, Pine Shadow Ranch. I slowed; the Bronco's high beams picked out a number of forms in the darkness: the ramshackle barn behind the house, a tilting windmill, a fractured swing dangling from one of the trees — and something on the ground.

I braked. I was so wired I was willing to believe my eyes were playing tricks, but as I waited there, the Bronco's engine idling, the thing on the ground showed no sign of disappearing.

Too tired to be cautious, I climbed out of the Bronco. It was no trick of light, no play of shadows. A man lay face down in the dirt.

I circled him, my footsteps unnaturally loud in the clear night. From across the yard I could hear a broken shutter banging. Wind rustled the tall winter grass. I knelt beside him.

I could see in the headlights that his face was turned to the side. His eyes were wide open, but he wasn't alive. His breath didn't cloud the raw air, his shoulders didn't rise and fall. There was a neat hole the size of a quarter between his shoulder blades.

I sucked in my breath. This wasn't my first contact with murder, but I still got that sensation of watching from a separate solar system — which usually precedes passing out cold. I rubbed my hand across my face. It was like one of those party games where you have thirty seconds to memorize a dozen objects; inevitably you see details instead of the big picture.

The dead man looked to be in his sixties maybe. His hair was thin, plastered to his head. He was grizzled, his fingernails were dirty. He wore faded jeans, a plaid flannel shirt and cowboy boots. I had never seen him before, or if I had I didn't recognize him.

Reaching out to touch his wrist, a shock rippled through me like I had not been properly grounded.

He was still warm.

I jerked my head up and stared at the silent house. I looked to the surrounding hills, the sentinel trees.

The wind whispered in the pines. Otherwise nothing moved. All was still. In fact ... too still.

Staring into the windswept darkness I became convinced someone was out there watching me. The hair prickled at the nape of my neck. My heart began to give my ribs the old one-two; a left and a right and then a left left left.

I don't have time for this, I warned my uncooperative ticker as I slammed back into the Bronco. Reversing in a wide arc, I put pedal to the metal, bumping and banging down the pothole-riddled road racing back the way I had come.

While I bounced along the road I felt around for my cell phone. Finding it at last, I dialed emergency.

It rang — and rang — and rang. Finally I got through to a sleepy someone in the Sheriff's Department. I opened my mouth and was instantly placed on hold. About one second before I spontaneously combusted, the line was picked up once more, and the voice, still sounding sleepy — had she dozed off the last time? — returned asking what the nature of my emergency was. After running through it a couple of times, she eventually seemed to understand what I was squawking about and promised to send help.

True to her word, the dispatcher sent the cavalry. A black-and-white, four-wheel drive met me at the mouth of Stagecoach Road twenty minutes later, lights flashing, siren blaring.

"What seems to be the trouble, sir?" The man in uniform was middle-aged, well-fed and a different species from the cops I'd come to know in the past few months.

I explained the trouble.

"Okay dokey," said Sheriff Billingsly, scratching his skunk-striped beard. "You hop in the truck and we'll go have a look-see at this alleged dead man."

I piled into the cab with the sheriff and his waiting deputy — Dwayne. Dwayne looked like he had just walked off the set of *Dukes of Hazzard*. He shifted his chaw to his other cheek.

"Howdy."

"Hi," I said through teeth starting to chatter with nerves.

Dwayne put the truck into gear and we headed back down the road.

"It was up here," I said as we clattered over the cattle guard. "Just outside the gate."

"Right along here?" the deputy asked, slowing as we approached the gate. The headlights fell on empty dirt road.

"Stop," I ordered. "It was along here that I found him."

The deputy braked hard and the three of us lurched forward and then back.

"Here?" the sheriff demanded.

The three of us stared at the lone tumbleweed somersaulting across the deserted yard.

"He was right there," I said.

Silence.

"Well he ain't there now," said the sheriff.

Made in the USA
Lexington, KY
10 July 2018